Leaving
EARTH

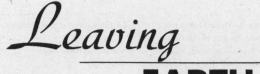

Leaving
EARTH

HELEN HUMPHREYS

HarperPerennial
HarperCollins*PublishersLtd*
A Phyllis Bruce Book

www.harpercanada.com

HarperCollins books may be purchased for
educational, business, or sales promotional
use. For information please write:
Special Markets Department,
HarperCollins Canada,
55 Avenue Road, Suite 2900,
Toronto, Ontario, Canada M5R 3L2

First HarperPerennialCanada edition

Canadian Cataloguing in Publication Data

Humphreys, Helen, 1961–
Leaving earth

"A Phyllis Bruce book"
ISBN 0-00-639184-2

I. Title

PS8565.U558L43 2001   C813'.54
C2001-901524-0
PR9199.3.H85L43 2001

RRD 9 8 7 6 5 4

Printed and bound in the United States

For the women who fly

T HE PLANE SLIPS from a spool of blue, stitches a confident loop in the sky. Willa stands by the hangar as the Moth roars above her head, growl of open throttle. The single figure in the rear cockpit waves as the plane flies low over the harbour airfield and then pulls up into a vertical climb. Up and up, the line so straight it could have been drawn with a ruler, could have been a harp string, the plane a note ascending.

At the top of the climb, the plane stalls, floats for a moment in the flap of blue and then falls towards earth.

Hammerhead.

Willa turns to the man beside her as the plane pulls out of its dive, throttles back and flies slowly over the hangar and off towards the islands. A scribble of smoke unravels behind it.

"Your wife?"

Jack drops his cigarette butt onto the ground, kicks it out with the toe of his boot.

"Yeah," he says. "That's my wife."

M ADDY RUNS along the sandbar in the shadow of the plane. Noise like gravel rattling in a wooden bowl. The underside of wings, dark blue tube of fuselage.

Moth.

Her breath pounds in her chest, in time with her running feet. The lake beside her is a thin blue ribbon wound tight around the trees at the water's edge.

The plane banks slowly left over the island and Maddy can see the open cockpits, the helmeted flyer hunched forward and leaning into the turn. She stops. The plane gathers above her, passes over. Scrape of wings against the flat sky. She lifts her small arms straight up.

"Grace O'Gorman," she yells into the rasp of engine. "Come back."

THE CANVAS BAG SWAYS as the fist jabs in, out, in again, right hand over left, gloves a blur in the low light. Sun riding sepia through the dusty windows of the hangar.

Left hook, thump. Push of exhale.

When the door opens, the light bunched up behind it rushes through so that Willa, sweat in her eyes, doesn't see the woman until she's crossed the concrete floor and is standing in front of her.

"Willa Briggs?"

Willa's hands fall to her sides. Her breath frays in the smooth air. There's the creak of the heavy bag lurching clumsy on its chain.

"I'm . . ."

"I know who you are," says Willa.

"Grace O'Gorman."

They both say it at the same time, the name chiming clear through the steel rafters.

Grace O'Gorman is dressed in her customary flying outfit: riding breeches and boots, long leather topcoat, leather gloves. Her cloth helmet and goggles are held at her side in her right hand. She's smaller than Willa had thought, but then she's never seen her this close before, just in the cockpit of her plane or standing distant on a stage. The famous aviatrix Grace

O'Gorman, skimming the heads of an audience to roll her blue Moth over on its left wing, the spike at the wing-tip spearing the white handkerchief spread carefully out on the field. The flutter of surrender in the blue sky.

"Will you walk with me?" says Grace, and Willa pulls off her boxing gloves, wipes her face on her sleeve and follows her through the hangar, empty except for a damaged Curtiss biplane.

Outside the sun is going down over the lake and islands. The air is warm, smells of gasoline.

"My husband tells me you live here," says Grace as they walk across the asphalt apron, away from the hangar and small cluster of buildings.

"I can't afford to live anywhere else," says Willa. "I don't have enough students."

"You don't get the lady trade?" asks Grace. "The girls whose fathers forbid them the potential charms of a male instructor?"

Silence.

"Isn't that how you met Jack?" says Willa.

Grace turns and smiles at her and Willa sees the eloquent dip of a wing, a white flash of acquiescence.

They walk across the apron, between the planes tied down to steel rings in the concrete, ropes lacing the space between wings and earth. Grace O'Gorman's blue Moth sits near Lake Ontario, at the end of the runway.

"Which way did you come in?" asks Willa.

"Lakeside," says Grace. "To land into the wind. It's a steady northerly."

Even so, thinks Willa, it's not enough to be a problem. Grace has put her plane down just feet from the water, meaning she was skipping across the tops of the waves. It would have been so much easier to drop from over the land. It's flat and empty around the little Air Harbour. There's nothing to get in the way.

"Do you know about my flight?" asks Grace, slowing down as they near her plane.

"The whole world knows about your flight," says Willa. The great Grace O'Gorman and Sally Tate, circling the Toronto harbour for twenty-five straight days. Refuelling in mid-air. Breaking the endurance record. And landing, on opening day, at the Canadian National Exhibition, to become an exhibit in front of the Automotive Building.

They have reached Grace's plane. It too seems smaller than Willa remembers. Moth DH60T. Biplane. Dark blue. Dual open-cockpit trainer. Two sets of controls, two sets of wings. Grace lays her gloved hand on an upper wing. It's a gesture of reassurance and Willa's not sure whom it's meant for — Grace or the plane itself.

"Sally Tate crashed at an air show yesterday. Broke a wrist. She's had to cancel on me." Grace traces an indistinguishable word onto the shiny fabric of the Moth wing. She watches her hand, doesn't look at Willa. "I saw you fly," she says. "Last year at the meet in Montreal."

Willa, having no plane of her own, had borrowed one from a member of the Toronto Flying Club. She hadn't placed in the race. Not where it counted, anyway.

"You were a little clumsy," admits Grace. "But you knew that air is fluid. You rode it like water." She turns and looks at Willa. "You knew what to do with it."

Willa just remembers the humiliation of coming seventh in a field of eleven women. She was banking too wide on the turns. Too cautious. Afraid of hurting the borrowed plane.

"I pancaked my landing." She remembers the embarrassing series of flat hops that had made her overshoot the runway.

"I don't care," says Grace. "I want you to take Sally Tate's place. Fly twenty-five days of circles. With me."

J ACK CLOSES the front door of their house, walks the hollow passageway to the kitchen. He's washing his hands when he hears the shift of floorboards above his head. He dries his hands on the curtains over the sink, runs his fingers through his hair, moves back into the hallway to call up the staircase.

"Grace."

"Hello, Robson." She looks down over the banister at him. "I'm back a day early. Sally broke her wrist."

Jack knows this. Fred had told him that afternoon. *You're off the hook. That Tate girl hurt herself.* He had shunted that knowledge home, a little way in front of him, periodically bumping up against it, feeling the solid comfort of relief.

Grace lays her head on her arms on the balustrade. "Oh, Robson," she says. "I'm so tired. How are you?"

"Worked on the Curtiss all afternoon," he says. "Wings are pretty banged up."

"Lessons?"

"Just two." Jack rests back against the wall. "Who can afford to fly when there's men in relief camps making twenty cents a day to dig holes and fill them in again."

Grace trails her hand through the wooden slats of the banister. "Come on, Robson," she says. "Come up here and lie down with me a while."

It's hot in the room upstairs, the sun pressing against the roof all day. The bed's by the open window, but the air outside hangs musty and still as an old curtain.

Jack takes his shirt and shoes off, lies on his back beside his wife, listens to the chuff and rumble of the street below. This is how he knows the world, he thinks. He prefers the look of it when he's fifteen hundred feet up and it's all tiny gasps of colour. But when he's down here, on the ground, he sifts his world through sounds. The sweep and shuffle of streetcars, the tick of traffic. The long, low moan of foghorns on the bay. It is the perfect combination, he thinks, as something clatters past beneath his window. To have the sounds of earth, but to be above it.

Grace bobs up against his shoulder, eyes closed. "I met one of your fellow instructors yesterday," she says sleepily.

"Yesterday?" Jack twists towards her. "You were back yesterday?"

"Flew out to Whitby after seeing Willa Briggs. I wanted Alex to look at the Moth one more time. Slept at Sally's. Flew back here today." Grace opens her eyes. "There's a lot to be done before I leave on Tuesday."

"Willa Briggs? Sally's . . ." Jack feels as if he's holding his breath, pushes it out into a noise that's the blunt edge of a sob.

They lie on their sides facing each other. Grace touches his cheek, moves her hand down to dust the outline of his collarbone. "Break it again, Robson," she whispers. "Let me have the record for a week or two and then come and get it back."

There's a hiss of tires on pavement outside. A moment later Jack hears the beginnings of rain on the roof. He looks at Grace. Air Ace Grace. How to tell her that she expects too much of him, that he's less capable than she thinks. He's not a natural. He can't set a record every year like she can. That eighteen-day endurance flight was the only real achievement of his aviation career. And now he's forty, too old to hang in the sky for a month.

"Will you still help me?" whispers Grace.

Jack watches the question in her eyes, deep blue, almost purple in the dusk. "A deal's a deal," he says.

Grace had flown the refuelling plane when he and Munro set the endurance record last year. It was only fair that he do the same for her. Only it wasn't fair. Every inch of his flying life had been scraped out of hard work, effort that nicked away his strength and confidence and left him less each time he flew. Air Ace Grace could fly so low it made your heart flicker. She could stunt blindfolded, barrel-rolling forty times in a row with a black bandanna tied tight across her eyes.

"Why are you doing this?" he says.

Grace takes her hand from his chest, flips over on her back. There's a seam of sweat on her upper lip, the flutter of rain on the roof. A strand of her red hair is stuck to her cheek. "Because, Robson," she says quietly, "I can take this record. I can make a perfect line across the month of August 1933. A perfect line in the sky."

M ADDY WAITS for her father outside their house. It's early
morning and the sun angles out of the lake, casting
thin wires of light onto the grass. She leans against the
wooden side wall, pops scales of old yellow paint off with her
thumbnail. In front of her is an open area of grass, a few trees.
Beyond that, the fresh concrete flat of the new and deserted
Air Harbour, levelling itself out to the small wooden lighthouse, on stilts, at the edge of the western gap. It is because
of the western gap, that small band of water between the
islands and the mainland, that the new Air Harbour is so far
unused. There is no way to get across the channel. Passengers
and pilots would have to traipse all the way along the western
sandbar, across the park to the Hanlan's Point ferry docks. It's
no small jaunt. So the new airport has been empty for over a
year, everyone still using the small Air Harbour on the mainland at the foot of Scott Street.

Maddy scowls across at the huge smooth of concrete.
What's the good of being the last house on the bar, of having
the perfect view of the airport, if there's nothing to see?

There's the bang of the front door. Maddy scoots around the
corner and falls into step with Fram as he heads down the narrow
street. She grabs his hand and swings it in slow arcs as they walk
past the rest of the houses on the bar, down towards the main

island and then to Hanlan's Point and the amusement park.

The Toronto Islands lie in the shape of a sickle moon, a bracket for the harbour, with the western sandbar at one tip and Ward's Island at the other. In between, nestled in the curve, are Centre Island, Mugg's Island, Olympic Island and Sunfish Island; all connected to each other or the main sweep of land by bridges. There are also several small, unnamed islands in the archipelago, as well as the peninsula of Hanlan's Point, sticking out like a thumb from the slender palm of the western sandbar.

Once there were Native encampments on the eastern side of the islands. In the 1800s, city dwellers came across in boats to set up tents and small cottages for summer use. Gradually a tent community evolved and ferries began regular crossings of the bay. By 1933, the only summer tent community left is on Ward's Island and, of the one hundred or so families who live on the islands year round, most have some form of wooden cottage and live on Centre Island, Hanlan's Point or the western bar. There is a grocery store on both Hanlan's Point and Ward's Island, but residents depend largely on the services of Centre Island's Manitou Road. Here can be found a butcher, grocery stores, a bank, drugstore, dairies and restaurants — including the pricey, elegant Pierson Hotel and the cheaper Honey Dew, which sells hamburger and frankfurter sandwiches.

Maddy and Fram walk down the narrow western sandbar, past the single furrow of houses, some fronting east, some facing west along the lake towards Hamilton. Each one planted with the same distance between it and the house next door. Each one painted a different colour, so that sometimes when Maddy rides fast past them on her bicycle the smudge of pinks and blues and yellows looks like the swirl at the bottom of a kaleidoscope.

Fram hums and Maddy listens, trying to guess the song. Sometimes they sing on the walk to work, songs they've learned from listening to Miro's new radiogram.

"'Stormy Weather'?" guesses Maddy and her father laughs and squeezes her hand.

Maddy's favourite songs are the musical tributes to the British aviatrix Amy Johnson, who flew a plane single-handedly from England to Australia in 1930. She kicks her feet through the dust on the road to the tune of "Queen of the Air" until she trips and Fram jerks her hard up by the arm to stop her from falling.

They walk up Hanlan's Point, along the sidewalk on Lake Shore Avenue, past the wooden houses and the church, over the grassy flat of park. They are the only people out this early. Squirrels. A dog with a limp skittering lopsided between the trees. Up ahead the rickety hill of "the Dips" offering glimpses of the amusement park through its trestles. The enclosed pavilion with refreshment bar and live-entertainment hall. The bumper cars and the Whip, Honeymoon Special, roller rink. The small wooden house of Miro, "King of All Fat Babies."

Maddy likes the amusement park best when it's deserted. A few ride operators there, like her father, to maintain and inspect the equipment. Some ducks and gulls pecking at bits of popcorn in the dirt. No noise and shudder of machinery. No hawkers. No crowds of people jostling and yelling; although there have been fewer people this summer than ever before. First it was the mainland amusement park at Sunnyside Beach that diminished the flow of people to Hanlan's. More recently it was the defection of the baseball team, the Maple Leafs, who moved from the athletic stadium on Hanlan's to a new stadium on the city side of the western gap. For the past few years there has been a substantial drop in human traffic and consequently a decrease in amusements. Ned the diving horse is gone. So too is the high wire and the giant swing. Hamburg's Big Spectacular Water Show isn't quite as big or spectacular, although Rose is still performing her popular matinee and evening show as "The Lady Who Takes Her Clothes Off Underwater." Now when Maddy and Fram walk across the expanse of the amusement park towards the ferry docks there are large gaps between exhibits and rides, spaces where things used to be. Everything its own island in the thick brown dust. Even her mother's booth, with the shiny tin stars and moon nailed to the outside walls and the words "Fortune Teller twenty-five cents" painted jauntily above the door, looks derelict. It used to stand in a row of booths, a shooting gallery on one side, a weight-guessing game on the other. Now it props up the emptiness, the sun flashing silver signals off its astral decorations.

All summer long Maddy's parents work the amusement park. Fram is at the merry-go-round from early in the morning until eleven at night. Del doesn't get to her fortune-teller's booth until noon. No one wants their future told first thing in the morning and Del's best trade is after sundown, when the dark makes people more inclined to ask the difficult questions. In the winter, when Maddy is back in her mainland school, they do odd jobs to get by. But last winter, with the Depression at its crest and over thirty per cent of the city's wage earners unemployed, there was nothing for either of them. No piece-work sewing for Del. No occasional engine repair for Fram. Maddy remembers the days and days of soup made from dried beans, the canned tomatoes in place of any fresh fruits and veg-etables. The talk, talk, talk of not enough.

Fram's merry-go-round sits between the figure-eight roller coaster and the ferry docks. On either side of it a wooden boardwalk stretches along the water's edge. The merry-go-round is a covered structure, built half on land, half over water on stilts sunk deep into the mud. The roof is red. The sides are open, so that when the carousel is flying fast it seems likely that one will spin off the wooden painted horses into the dirty water of the bay.

Maddy takes her seat on her favourite mount, a large black horse with lips drawn back in a snarl, the bright red of gums, white of bared teeth. Fram turns the key in the operator's box, moves the motion lever a fraction so that the horses begin a slow roll around the perimeter while he busies himself fetching oil can and rags from a locked wooden chest.

This is how it is every morning in the summer. Maddy rides the fierce black horse while her father oils the bearings, polishes the metal stirrups on the real leather saddles. Like a lazy wave of water the carousel tumbles forward through the still morning air.

"Maddy. Hold the reins together." Fram keeps pace with her as the pack of horses rises up and down over the water. He used to ride when he was a boy in Scotland and sometimes he gives his daughter lessons on the stiff, wooden stallions that gallop forever in a circle. He never turns the music on in the early mornings and there's just the creak of cogs, the exhale as the horses drop down on their poles. "Stand up a little on the balls of your feet."

Fram taps Maddy's heel with the spout of his oil can and she lifts herself up in the smooth saddle.

"It feels tippy," she says and reaches out for his shoulder to steady herself.

"It's not a chair," says Fram.

He narrows his eyes against the light sliding sharp across the water. "You're riding rough up in the scrag. Your horse . . ."

"Amelia," says Maddy.

"Your horse, Amelia," continues Fram, "is unsteady through the shift of rock. She is picking her way along, mindful of hurting herself."

"If she breaks her leg, I'll have to shoot her," says Maddy cheerfully.

"Never mind that," says Fram. "She can't be breaking her leg. She's all you've got. How will you get out to hunt up food for your wee ones?"

Maddy pulls up hard on Amelia's reins. "I don't want wee ones," she says. "You keep getting it all wrong. I'm riding out over my property. Just to look at all my things. I have lots of food already. I have," she says pointedly, "oranges."

Fram sighs. His daughter's hand is a hot point on his shoulder. There are already boats on the slippery lake. "Whose story is this?" he says.

Maddy bares her teeth at him from atop her wooden horse. "Mine," she says, without any hesitation.

WILLA COILS her left hand back against her chin, unleashes it into Simon's glove. Pulls it in again, pushes forward, her body sideways so that her arm comes out straight from the shoulder.

"Move your feet," says Simon. "Like this." He drops down and lunges across the floor of the hangar, left fist snapping in and out like the head of a striking snake. "Heel then toe then arm. Your punch should be just a little slower than your feet."

Willa wipes her forehead with her arm, shuffles forward trying to imitate Simon; fails. "Sorry," she says.

It's hot in the hangar. Air stuffy as the thick feather insides of a pillow.

"Have a rest," says Simon.

Willa removes her gloves and sloshes water from a thermos into her mouth. Her hands are stained black from the dye in the gloves. "Maybe we'll start *your* lessons," she says. "When I come down from the endurance flight. September."

Simon rocks back on his heels, raises his arms out from his sides. "The flying boxer," he says. "Couldn't hurt. Maybe it will change my luck, help me win a few matches."

"You almost always win," says Willa. She quotes a recent newspaper headline. "'Simon Kahane, Fastest Fists in the City.'"

"That would be *Jew* fists," says Simon, pulling off his gloves. "Know how they've got my fight against O'Brien set?"

Willa passes him the thermos and he dumps what's left of the water over his head.

"The Hebe against the Mick," says Simon. "Last week it was the Evil Jew against the Italian. Well," he says, "I'm going to play into their stupid race war. I got my sister Del to stitch a Star of David onto my fighting trunks. Just like Max Baer."

In June the Jewish boxer Max Baer had beaten the German boxer Max Schmeling. Baer had won a technical knockout in the tenth round. He had fought with a Star of David sewn onto his boxing trunks.

"It happens to me too," says Willa. "'The Weaker Sex in First Powderpuff Air Derby.'"

"'Two Girls Circle the Toronto Islands,'" quotes Simon. "'Can They Last 25 Days?'"

Willa practises her jab against the heavy canvas bag with her bare fists. "The big question," she says, moving in and out, heel-toe and back, heel-toe and back, "is whether or not we're going to wear lipstick up there."

Simon grins. "And are you?"

"No," says Willa, following her left with a right and then coming in with the satisfying hammer of the hook. "We're most definitely not."

Simon watches her box the heavy bag. She's got strength and power, Willa Briggs. Needs to work on her speed. "Up there the worst thing will be the cramped space," he says. "You could do a bit of punching to keep yourself loose. Especially punching off to the side so you twist your upper body at the waist." He demonstrates, throwing punches while moving his torso from side to side.

Willa has thought a lot about the limited movement that awaits her in the plane. She has been trying to come up with ways to exercise in the small cockpit of the Moth. Some of the boxing techniques will work well for her shoulders and arms, but what she's worried about most are her legs. When she's doing the flying they will get a bit of work moving the rudder pedals, but otherwise they will be tucked into the fuselage, immobile and getting weaker by the day. There have been so few endurance flights that there's no one to ask about the conditions aloft for such a long time. There's only Jack Robson, husband of Grace O'Gorman and the man whose record they're trying to shatter. This morning Willa sat in the rear cockpit of the wrecked Curtiss biplane, twisting her body into awkward contortions, trying to imagine what levels of discomfort she will have to endure over the coming month. "Can They Last 25 Days?" Willa is not sure. She doesn't doubt their flying ability (well, not Grace's, anyway), or the mechanics of the plane. What she is concerned about is what will happen to the part of themselves that they are making obsolete by being airborne — the earthbound legs with their memory of walking, their blind service to gravity.

WILLA STOPS for a moment outside Grace's house. She's breathing fast and wants to calm her nervousness before she steps up the walk and knocks on the door.

It's early evening. A warm breeze lifts and lowers the leaves on the tree just inside the wooden gate. Linden. Willa can smell the night scent of flowers. Roses.

The street is empty except for three boys at the far end, playing noisily with a stick and tin can. The smack and rattle of two objects coming together. Laughter and running feet.

Grace's house is so ordinary. Brick and windows. Attached on the left to an identical house. *Worker's house*, says the critical voice of Willa's mother inside her head. Out-of-worker's house. Sure, Jack puts in hours at the airfield as a flight instructor and, like Willa, earns a pittance, but Air Ace Grace must be rich. All the races she's won, records she's set. Willa tries not to be disappointed with the house, but she'd been counting on a fancy one. Marble and rugs from India. A grand piano with a shiny black surface that reflected a face back clear as a mirror.

Grace answers on the third set of knocks, as though she's come from somewhere far beyond the confines of the small house. She looks tired, holds the door open and ushers Willa inside without a word. There are no lights on and Willa bumps along behind Grace into the parlour, afraid of tripping over something or banging hard into a wall. Even in the dark of the room, Willa can see the shiny silver line of trophies on the mantel. Cups and statues of women with their arms raised. Silver wreaths of never-fading flowers.

"These are all yours?" she says, before she can stop herself from sounding stupid.

Grace looks over to the fireplace.

"Oh those," she says vaguely. "Bits of tin I picked up here and there. Iced tea?"

She doesn't wait for a reply, leaves the room. Willa, not knowing whether to stay in the dark parlour or follow to the kitchen, hesitates for a few moments and then lurches after Grace down the narrow hallway.

"What are you doing here?" asks Grace, surprised, turning at the kitchen doorway. "Oh well, have to get used to this, I guess. We've got twenty-five days of it to go. Come on."

They take the pitcher of iced tea and glasses out through the kitchen door to the back garden, sit on wooden chairs on a small stone patio near the house. Grace lights several candles on the table between them. Beyond the orange splash of light Willa can see the shapes of bushes, the bent heads of flowers.

There is silence.

"Right," says Grace. "Enough pleasantries. I want to warn you about the parachutes."

"What parachutes?" says Willa. She jerks her glass of iced tea too sharply from the table and spills a little on her good slacks.

"No parachutes," says Grace firmly. "I want to keep the weight down. Already with the oversize fuel tank we're in trouble."

"In trouble?"

"Well, not in trouble, exactly. Just close to the edge. The lip of the abyss."

Willa thinks that Grace might be smiling, but she can't see properly in the candlelight. No parachutes. What if something happens up there and they need to escape from the plane? Willa's hands start to shake. She puts down her glass carefully, afraid it might slide right out of her grip.

Grace leans forward over the candles, her pale skin slick with light. "If I want a record, I do what's necessary to get it. I haven't failed yet."

Willa, who has mostly failed at her few attempted air races, finds Grace's confidence so far out of her experience that she can't help but believe her. "Okay," she says, meaning the parachutes.

Grace waves her hand lightly through the air. The candle flame flickers. "Like an angel," she says. "I can fly like an angel."

Willa remembers seeing that as a headline once: "Grace O'Gorman Flies Like an Angel." "Okay," she says again.

"Fay Weston thought she had me in the cross-country hop last year." Grace drops her arm and looks straight at Willa. "But I outfoxed her in the final hundred miles and took the race. Flew above the clouds so she didn't know I was there until it was too late."

"You always do win everything," says Willa.

"That makes it sound so easy," says Grace. She looks carefully at Willa. "How old are you?"

"Twenty-three."

"When I was your age I had to beg to be taken up. No one would do it, except for Jack Robson. A woman flyer! Not possible. Now ten years later, look how air-minded everyone's become. Look how easy it's been for you to be a pilot."

"It hasn't been easy for me," says Willa.

"All right," concedes Grace. "Not easy, but possible."

Willa drinks some of her iced tea. The ice has melted and it tastes watery. "I used to cut your picture out of magazines," she says. "When I was younger. I made a scrapbook."

"And do you still have it?"

Willa doesn't want to admit that she does, and worse, even knows exactly where it is — on the bookshelf by the window in her cabin. "I might have it stashed somewhere," she says casually.

Grace smiles. "Well," she says, "that's very flattering. There'll be lots more to add to your little book after this flight." She pauses. "Were they *good* pictures of me? The ones you cut out?"

Willa feels nervous again, wishes she'd never mentioned the scrapbook. She seems to amuse Grace and she's not sure why. "Can't remember," she says. "There were lots of shots of the plane."

"Good old Moth," says Grace with real affection. "This will be another record for that plane. You don't mind, do you?"

"Mind what?"

"Taking the Moth. It's the plane I always use. It's my plane."

"I don't mind," says Willa. And she doesn't. "I like open cockpits. It doesn't feel like flying to be shut away inside a cabin."

"Good." Grace sounds pleased. "I'm sorry about the parachutes. Hope it doesn't make you nervous. But they're just so bulky. And it's so much better to have the big fuel tank. To minimize contact with the refuelling plane."

"Jack," says Willa.

"What?"

"Jack is the refuelling plane, isn't he? And it's Jack's record we're trying to break."

"It's Jack's record. For now." There's something very hard in Grace's voice. Willa remembers someone telling her once that no one was allowed to get the better of Grace O'Gorman. That she liked to put people in their place. And their place was always way down below hers.

And me too, thinks Willa. That means me too.

There's a shuffling noise from the house and Willa turns to see Jack, backlit by the kitchen.

"There you are," he says.

"Hello, Robson." Grace looks over at her husband slouched against the doorframe.

"She telling you what to do," says Jack to Willa.

"What to *bring*," says Grace firmly.

"Ah." Jack stands there for a moment. No one says anything.

A breeze brushes Willa's face. She can smell the flowers out there in the dark. Night roses. No more of that, she thinks. Up in the plane there will be no scent of earth. No deep, rich loam of summer. Willa can imagine it gone, what ties her to this world. She can see this scene without them. Empty chairs. The dark garden. And higher, the peak of the roof, then the thick length of the street with its bulge of houses at the sides. And finally a place where there is just the cold light of heaven, black slab of night.

"Anything you want to ask me?"

Willa looks up, startled. Grace stares at her over the candles. Jack is gone.

"Ask me anything."

It seems to Willa as if this is something she's been waiting her whole life to hear. *Ask me anything.* What is it she needs to know?

Somewhere a cat cries. Or a baby. Willa feels herself float up over the garden again, over the bright sparking candles, the top of Grace's head.

We're somewhere else already, she thinks. What holds us here has let us go. What she needs to know from Grace is how to come back.

After Willa has left, Jack brings two beers outside, hands one to Grace. He sits down opposite her. "So?" he says.

Grace sighs. "Oh, Robson. She's young enough to have kept a scrapbook of my flights."

Jack snorts with laughter. "Grace, Grace. Willa Briggs *is* young." He means inexperienced and Grace knows this.

"But she'll be fine," she says breezily.

"And what if she screws up? What if she can't take the physical strain of being in the air for that long? What if she wants to come down?"

"She won't." Grace puts her beer bottle on the table. "I can make her stay up there."

"How?"

"I'll think of something."

"Well, good luck to you, girl." Jack leans back in his chair, breathes in the heavy musk of the garden. "What I see is a young pilot who wants to please you. How many days is that going to buy?"

"**D**ON'T SIT ON THAT. If you've got grease on that monkey suit of yours I don't want it all over the davenport."

Willa, in the process of lowering herself to the cushions, rises awkwardly back up again. "Mother. These are my *good* clothes."

Mrs. Briggs flings a doily down on the mahogany end table nearest her daughter. "Only on this. You put your cup down only on this."

The tea hasn't even been poured yet. The pot sweats under a cosy on the tray. Two china cups and saucers. Willow pattern.

Mrs. Briggs plucks at Willa's sleeve. "Let me get you a towel."

"A towel?"

"To sit on."

Her mother hurries from the room as though it's burning. Willa grits her teeth and resists the urge to drop-kick the teapot across the immaculate living room. Doilies, she thinks bitterly. There are doilies under the jade carriage clock on the mantel, under the porcelain figurines. Doilies under crystal ashtrays and empty candy dishes. Doilies for display. Some places there are even doilies under doilies. The small cluttered house is a doily museum. All made by her mother. Days and nights of careful, tiny stitches, sitting in the wing-back chair next to the good light.

Mrs. Briggs rushes back into the room, carrying what Willa recognizes as the "dog towel," formerly used for wiping the delicate muddy feet of her mother's long-dead poodle, Mr. Tippet.

"This is so much better," says Mrs. Briggs, smoothing the towel into the curve of the sofa cushions. "Now you just sit right back and I'll pour us a nice cup of tea. I'm sure you haven't had a proper cup of tea since the last time you visited. When was that now? That last time you were here to see your mother? Could it have been as much as a month ago, even though you've promised to come every week? My goodness, time does rush along, doesn't it?"

"For heaven's sake," says Willa fiercely. "I can make myself a stinking cup of tea."

There is a brief silence. Willa can feel the crustiness of the dog towel through her thin slacks.

"Well," says Mrs. Briggs finally. "That's what's to be expected, I suppose, living in that airport. Filth like that springing from your lips."

"The lips of the abbess," mutters Willa.

"Pardon?"

"Nothing." Willa squirms on the towel. It is no good saying anything in her defence. She knows better than to try that. "Listen, Mother," she says. "I've come to tell you that I won't be by for the next little while. For the next month, actually. You see, I . . ." She stops, starts again. "Remember that woman pilot who set the altitude record last year, Grace O'Gorman?"

Mrs. Briggs shucks the embroidered cosy from the ironstone teapot. "That crazy woman with ice on her face when they brought her down?"

This is not quite true. Grace, wearing an insulated leather "teddy bear" suit, had flown her plane straight up to thirty-five thousand feet, a height where the cold numbed her body so severely she could barely operate the controls of the plane, a height at which oxygen deprivation made her confused and weak and the air was too thin for the engine of the Moth. Dropping back down to the thick, soupy air of earth, she had frostbite on her nose and cheeks when they pulled her stiff padded body from the plane.

"Not ice, Mother. Frostbite."

"Careful with this now." Mrs. Briggs hands Willa a cup of tea. "You know how you are with things."

Willa ignores the remark, takes the cup and puts it carefully down on top of the end-table doily. "Grace O'Gorman is going to set an endurance record this year. Twenty-five days of flying around the harbour. In-air refuelling. She has asked me to fly this with her and I have said yes."

"What have I done to you that you should hate me so much as to do these things?" Mrs. Briggs puts a napkin up to dab the tears from her eyes that haven't appeared yet. "All I did was to raise you properly. A thankless task. All alone. A poor, bereft widow."

"You're not a widow," says Willa.

"Well, I might as well be," snaps her mother. She no longer anticipates weeping, puts her napkin neatly back on her lap.

"Grace O'Gorman is famous," says Willa. "If this flight works, if we set a record, it will raise my profile as a flyer. It will help my career."

"You don't have a career," says her mother. "You have a sickening obsession. An illness."

Willa picks up her cup and slurps from it, on purpose,

watching her mother's face twitch with disapproval. "It's done," she says. "I'm going."

"Well, if she's so famous, this Grace O'Gormless, why did she ask you to go with her?"

"I'm a replacement."

"Of course you are."

Willa slams her cup and saucer down on the doily-covered table. Don't do this, she thinks. Just tell her and leave. Don't play this game. "Her regular partner broke a wrist. There aren't that many women with their pilot's licence. I was handy."

Mrs. Briggs is quiet for a moment. Willa can hear the well-oiled tick of the carriage clock on the mantel behind her.

"Twenty-five days?" says her mother.

"Twenty-five days."

"Well then, you'd better go up and see about my bedroom window. It's sticking again. I might suffocate to death by the time you make it back here."

Willa stands on the upstairs landing. This is where she comes from — this woman, this house. This is the hall where she wasn't allowed to play jacks, wasn't allowed to roll a rubber ball down its waxed wooden length. Over there is the bedroom where she would lie awake nights, listening to her mother breathing noisily in the next room. The bedroom that was always cold, though not as cold as the bathroom, where her mother insisted on leaving the window open, summer and winter, because of germs. The habits of germs. Willa knows these better than the names of flowers or the nations of the world. This is what she has learned from her mother: Make sure you always damp mop the ceiling, do the housework with gloves on, shake hands firmly. Pretend that you have never loved anyone, that they're dead or about to die any day. Don't ever say what you mean. Don't know what it is you feel. Don't feel.

Willa reaches a hand out to touch the flat of the wall. "Goodbye," she says, her voice hollow in the still air.

S IMON PULLS ASIDE the heavy blanket over the doorway of the fortune-telling booth and enters the dark interior. A candle burns on a small covered table, bounces light off a crystal ball. A woman with a scarf tied around her head is shuffling a deck of cards. She looks up at the brief triangle of daylight that forms in the entranceway.

"Hi, Del," says Simon, sitting down on the stool across from her. "How's business?" He fishes into a pocket of his jacket. "I bought us a couple of sandwiches on the way over. Cheese."

Del reaches across the dark blue tablecloth with the sewn-on silver moons and takes the offered paper packet. "Thanks," she says. "At least eating will be something to do."

Simon rustles through his other pocket, pulls out a length of gauze, drops it on the table in front of his sister. "O'Brien's hand wrap," he says. "Took it when he was in having a shower after training yesterday."

Del pokes at it with a finger. "I don't want to hold some sweaty, stinky bandage," she says.

"It's the best I can do, Del," says Simon. "I can't exactly steal his ring or his coat."

They chew in silence for a few moments. Simon shifts his weight on the stool. There are thin bars of light between the slats of the wall behind his sister. "Come on, Del," he pleads. "It's this week."

Del sighs and, still holding the sandwich in her right hand, picks up the pile of gauze with her left. She squeezes it, closes her eyes. There's the sound of a ferryboat horn from out on the bay, the bray of a gull from close by the booth. "He's not a happy man," says Del. "He's got big regrets and he blames himself for a lot of things. A lot of things that happened when he was young."

"The fight," says Simon impatiently. "What about the fight?"

Del bows her head over the tapeworm of gauze. "He's not ready. He doesn't have the confidence to beat you. Something . . ." She suddenly looks up at Simon. "Soft. He's soft. You've got to hit him in the body. The belly and the ribs. Keep coming in on him. You'll wear him down. He won't be able to take the beating."

Simon slaps the tabletop so hard that the crystal ball pops up out of its socket and rolls into his lap. He scoops it up as he stands and walks to the doorway. Tosses it underhand back to Del, who catches it. "Thanks," he says, his hand on the rough weave of blanket.

"Wednesday," says Del. "You'll feed Maddy her supper, fetch her home?"

Her brother waves his hand in agreement and flicks the blanket aside to exit, as if he's flinging off a cape from around his shoulders.

Del watches the blank of the entranceway after he's gone, and then, lowering her gaze back to the table, brushes crumbs slowly onto the dirt floor of the booth.

Simon sees Maddy over by the ferry docks. She's standing at the edge of the boardwalk, leaning into the wooden railing, watching two men fish beside her. She's concentrating on the still line of their rods so intently that she doesn't see Simon at all. He has to tap her on the head to get her attention.

"Hey there," he says. "I'm coming for you Wednesday night. Be at your mother's booth by seven."

Maddy scowls at him. "I can go home by myself," she says. "I do it every day."

"Thursday's my fight," says Simon. "I'm sleeping over at your place on Wednesday." He drops down into his stance and playfully jabs at her shoulder. "Big fight."

Maddy jerks out of his way and Simon straightens up.

"Your mother wants me to come get you. Feed you supper." He feels like saying, *It's not my fault*, but stops himself. Maddy used to be such a good kid. He used to like spending time with her. She would listen to him, ask him things, box with him. Now he's no longer her hero. He's been replaced with all those Queens of the Air. "Hey," he says, suddenly remembering. "That endurance flight of Grace O'Gorman's isn't going to have Sally Tate in it any more. She broke a bone."

"What?" Maddy turns to him. "How do you know?"

"Because," says Simon, leaning right over the railing to stare into the brown water that licks up against the wood. "I traded boxing lessons for flying lessons with a young lady pilot at the Air Harbour. Willa Briggs. She's going to be the new Sally Tate."

"Take me to a lesson," begs Maddy. "Let me see her. I don't have any pictures of that one. I need to look at her." She grabs onto his sleeve but he shakes her off.

"Missed your chance," he says. "Today was the last lesson for a while. Tomorrow they take off." He starts walking away, turns back after a few feet. "Wednesday," he says firmly, "you be outside your mother's booth at seven o'clock. I'll be coming for you and I don't want to have to wait. I've got an important fight to get ready for, you know."

GRACE AND JACK are at the airfield, in the small office at the back of the hangar. Grace is perched on the edge of the big wooden desk with Jack sitting behind it. She is in overalls, holds a clipboard against her knee. Her legs are crossed and she swings the top one up and down, slowly.

"The girl won't be at the dinner tonight," she says. "The one from the *Almanac* who's organizing the drops. She can't come until Tuesday. She's to have a cabin to run her operation from. It's been cleared." She pulls the top piece of paper from her clipboard and hands it to her husband. "I want you to give her this list. It's all the food I like. What I'm going to want to eat up there."

Jack takes the paper, scans it. "What about Willa Briggs? Have you asked her what she wants to eat?"

"Oh, Willa Briggs will be happy with anything," says Grace. "Tell that *Almanac* girl there's to be no ham. Ever. In any form. You know how I despise it."

Jack sighs and lays the paper on the desk. He leans back in his chair. "They're paying for this, right?"

"Food and fuel," says Grace. "Anything else comes out of my pocket. Fuel for the plane you'll use. Wages for the man who's going to help you with the food drop. You have arranged that, haven't you? I need to make this record so I can afford to pay for it all. No one realizes how expensive it is. How broke I am. But if I fly sweet and it all comes through, I'm bound to get a big sponsorship after this."

"You could have done distance again," says Jack.

"I wanted to stay home."

"Speed."

"I just did that one."

Jack shakes his head. "Grace, this is mine."

"Well, break it back then," she says impatiently. She sees his face. "Robson, I can do this, that's why I'm doing it. It's not about you."

But it is, thinks Jack. Only she will never say it. She has to better everyone, even her own husband, the one who taught her all of this. But really, thinks Jack, if I am honest, she *is* better than all of us, than anyone. And this, though he doesn't often admit it, is partly why he loves her. She is what he isn't, what he wanted to have been.

"Come on," he says, standing up. "We're going to be late for your big do. We have to get home and change."

"Never enough time," says Grace. "Sally gave me money to get my fortune told before we leave. For luck. There's supposed to be a good fortune-teller at Hanlan's. But it all gets so crazy before a flight."

She takes Jack's offered hand and he spins her off the desk. They walk out into the hangar, their footsteps tapping after them.

"Bit like a church, isn't it," says Jack. "The echo. How the sound just goes on and on, gets folded over and starts again."

"I'm not trying to hurt you," says Grace.

"I know that." Jack squeezes her hand. "In my better moments, I know that."

She could have had anyone, Grace O'Gorman, but she chose her flight instructor. She chose him. He knows that some people think she married him only because she wanted continuous access to his knowledge and experience, wanted connection to the planes and facilities of the Air Harbour. But he would have given her that anyway. On Jack's better days he knows that Grace needs him, needs his stability and common sense, wants to be around someone who knew her long before she was Air Ace Grace, the celebrity. And he knows that she is not malicious, is out to break his record simply because it's the only one she doesn't have. But it still feels like a betrayal. And Jack almost wishes that he'd been like everyone else when the young stenographer had come asking for lessons, that he too had said, "No, I can't teach you to fly. It's not something women should do."

They walk through the hangar and outside. The moon is over the water. This is a good place to be right now, thinks Jack. Down here, on the ground. Beyond them the tethered planes are dark jagged shapes. The hangar rises and rises. Jack puts an arm around his wife. She still carries her clipboard, he can feel it in her hand.

"What are you thinking about?" he asks.

"The flight." She turns her face towards him, sees his disappointment. Her voice is quiet. "Oh, Robson. What was it you wanted me to say?"

THE FAREWELL DINNER for Grace is at a fancy downtown hotel. A place Jack has never been. He finds it hard to reconcile the glittering interior with the men on the streets outside holding cardboard signs that say "Will Work for Food." But he goes inside.

Grace's flight is being sponsored by the *Adventure Girl Almanac*, a popular magazine for young women that publishes illustrated stories of feminine heroic deeds. The Moth will have *Adventure Girl* stencilled on the fuselage before it goes aloft and becomes a circling, flying advertisement for the magazine. In return for the costs of food and fuel and a staffer to work out of the airfield, cooking for Grace and Willa, handling any supply requests and organizing the food drops, Grace has agreed to let the *Almanac* tell the story of the flight. They will have exclusive rights to coverage and upon the completion of the endurance flight will devote an entire issue to it and other noteworthy exploits of Air Ace Grace.

The dinner is a cosy affair. Mr. Dalton, publisher of the *Almanac* is there, as well as Maud Spencer, the writer, and Ned Stockwell, the illustrator. Mr. Dalton's secretary is present, just introduced as Mary, and Councillor Piper from city hall. Jack is certain that he wasn't really invited and that Grace has just brought him along regardless.

"Where's Willa Briggs?" he asks Grace, as they're being ushered into the dining room.

"Where's Willa Briggs?" says Grace to Mr. Dalton.

"Who?" Mr. Dalton has his hand firmly on Grace's elbow, as though she can't manoeuvre herself through the blockade of tables and chairs.

She could fly right through you, thinks Jack.

Grace stops. Some of the party are in the process of being seated. The remaining one or two stop behind Grace.

"Willa Briggs," she says. "The other woman who will be up in the plane for twenty-five days. Risking her life."

Mr. Dalton shifts uncomfortably and looks around for his secretary, but she's already seated at the table.

"Uh," he says. "It must have been an oversight. We, uh, knew you were getting a replacement for Sally, but we didn't know who it was."

Grace is not impressed with this. "You could have asked," she says.

For one wild moment Jack feels like volunteering to go and find Willa Briggs and bring her here. Anything to get him out of this place, away from these people. But Willa Briggs would be so bad at this, he thinks. She would be as bad as he is at all the polite lies. His impulse to find Willa recedes into relief that she's not there, that she's been spared this dinner, this moment.

The table they sit at is large and round. Grace is seated between Mr. Dalton and Councillor Piper. Jack, on the other side, sits next to Ned, the illustrator, and Mary, the secretary. The writer, Maud Spencer, sits between Councillor Piper and Ned. Drinks are ordered and served. Small talk is attempted, abandoned and attempted again. Jack notices that Ned is sketching something on his drink napkin.

"To be a bird," says Councillor Piper feverishly. "To skim the heads of those on this mortal earth. To taste freedom."

"It will be exhaust," says Grace, "that we'll be tasting."

Jack sees that Ned is drawing Grace. A few quick strokes for her face. The line of neck to shoulder that Jack knows so well.

"But surely," blusters Councillor Piper, reluctant to surrender his wings, "soaring is about having feathers."

Maud Spencer stirs her scotch in small, tidy circles. "Perhaps," she says, "flying to a bird is like walking to us."

"Well, what's the point then," says Mary, so bitterly that everyone turns and looks at her. She lowers her head and fiercely reads the menu.

No one has an answer.

"I hope," offers Mr. Dalton, recovering his natural charm. "I hope that Grace will allow us all the chance to see what it is like above the clouds."

Rides. Jack knows that Grace hates giving rides, especially in a plane that has dual controls. It is so easy for someone, buoyed up by the sensation of being in the air, to feel reckless with confidence and want to see what happens if he moves the stick or presses a button, pulls a lever.

Grace leans back in her chair. "Of course," she says, "I would be delighted to give rides when the endurance flight is done. But you should be aware of the danger."

"Danger?" Councillor Piper leans in. They all lean in, even Ned, who's trying to sketch Grace's hands while they're in motion. Jack recalls one of the *Adventure Girl Almanac*'s covers from the complimentary pile that arrived for Grace to look through. A nicely drawn colour picture of a mountain peak. Three figures visible near the top, with walking sticks and large packsacks strapped to their backs. The headline in red across the crest of the mountain: AVALANCHE PERIL! Neither he nor Grace had gone on to read the story.

"Planes crash a lot," says Grace bluntly. "A pilot will probably crash more than once during her career. She might die. She might not. I myself have made a few forced landings and cracked open a few planes."

And always walked away from them, thinks Jack.

"Last year," Grace says, "a woman I know, a pilot, gave a man a ride at a local fair. This was how she financed her flying, by giving rides. Moth, like mine. She was flying back to the fairground from low over the lake and the man, who was quite a large gentleman, wanted to get a better view of the water. He leaned over the side of the cockpit at the same moment she was banking slightly in the direction of his lean. The plane wing dipped with the extra weight and the tip caught the water. The Moth flipped over on its back. The pilot was knocked out and because she was strapped in by her harness, hanging upside down in the water, she drowned. The passenger wasn't wearing his harness. They think he'd taken it off during the flight. He spilled out when the plane went over. But he died anyway. Heart failure at the shock of the crash."

There is a silence while they all consider this.

"Couldn't she have saved them?" asks Maud quietly.

Jack thinks of another *Adventure Girl Almanac* cover: GIRL SAVES TOWN FROM FIRE! "Couldn't she have warned him of what might happen?"

"There is no warning," says Grace. "We never think it will happen to us, or else we'd stay on the ground."

Jack recognizes the truth of this and looks up from his drink to his wife looking across at him. She smiles and he suddenly forgives her everything.

Councillor Piper turns to Grace. "I am not a large man," he says triumphantly.

GRACE WALKS ACROSS the concrete apron of the airfield to where her plane is tied down, last in the line of planes, close to the lake. It's early evening, the day before the endurance flight is to begin. Grace is ostensibly here to check on the Moth. At least that's what she told Jack before she left the house.

The sun is still up, propping open the western horizon beyond the islands. A sky of pale pink. The same colour as the roses in my garden, thinks Grace. She stands beside the wings of the Moth, puts a hand up to feel along the edge of the top one. There's nobody else about at the airfield. No one from the press she has to talk to. No passer-by inquiring politely about the flight, asking for an autograph.

"Just you and me, old thing," says Grace to the plane, moving around to the fuselage, leaning her body against the metal near the front cockpit. "You and me again."

She's been feeling jumpy all day, out of her skin. Couldn't sit still, settle to anything. Now she is beginning to return to her normal self again. If the Moth hadn't been fuelled up for tomorrow, she would take it for a spin right now. Fly out over the islands and check the route. Maybe scoot out to Hamilton and come back in the dark, following the glowing curve of lights from the shore. It would feel so good to be up in the sky again by herself. No one understands what that is. Sally. Maybe Willa Briggs, she thinks, releasing the front cockpit door, stepping onto the wing and climbing up and in. Well, we'll soon see about that. She doesn't want to admit it to Jack but she is worried about Willa's inexperience. There was so little time to find a replacement if the flight was to stay on schedule that there really was no one else to choose from. She'll have to babysit Willa and she's not looking forward to that. The main thing will be keeping the young pilot alert and functional so she doesn't make a mistake and crash them both.

Grace pulls the door flap closed. It is odd to be sitting in a quiet and stationary plane. It is all she's ever wanted, to fly, and try as she does she can't help feeling that everything else is a poor substitute for being in the sky. She wasn't totally honest with Jack. She wants to try an endurance flight partially because she wants to see what it feels like to stay up for a long time, to see how long she can stay up. If this is where she's happiest and most herself, then what will it be like to fly non-stop for almost an entire month? Will she look at her life on the ground differently? Will she miss it? Or will she just confirm what she already secretly knows, that she was meant to live up, high up, above the earth.

There are times, when Grace is flying blindfolded or upside down, that she is doing everything by feel. Instinct and knowing. And it has taken years, her whole life, to learn the simplest subtleties. She has no need for instruments. She's learned how the plane flies from listening to the plane. The whine of the wind in the rigging wires, how she can tell what speed she's going by the pitch of that sound. The more she does something, the more fixed in her it becomes. She has probably pulled the nose of the Moth up by hauling back on the stick thousands and thousands of times, and that feeling of the stick under her hand, that short distance it travels back, are so familiar that they exist in her body now, in the memory of her body. That distance the stick comes back is the length of measurement she unconsciously uses for the space she stands away from someone she's talking to. That feel of the stick under her hand, the pressure she uses to pull her arm back, is the same pressure she uses when she touches Jack's skin, runs a hand over his naked back. It's hard to tell anyone this, to make it understood that she doesn't really fly the plane. The plane flies her.

It's fully dark when Grace climbs down out of the Moth. There are lights visible from the amusement park on Hanlan's Point. She's tempted to get on a ferry and go over there. Ride the Dips. Have her fortune told. But no, she turns from the lake and walks back to where her car is parked beside the hangar. She has to go home and think of something nice to say to Jack so he won't be so disappointed with her. So he'll do a good and thorough job of running the refuelling drops. All the little tricks and concessions, she thinks, giving a last backward glance at the Moth. Just so I'm allowed to use the gift the Fates gave me.

WILLA, IN HER CABIN behind the hangar, sits in her bathtub and thinks of all the things she'll have to do without for the next twenty-five days. Baths for one, although Grace has said they can *wash* with rubbing alcohol. Stretching her legs, she thinks, looking down at them in the water. It is possible to stand up in a biplane, but there will be a forceful backdraft from the propeller and she'll have to watch she doesn't get toppled overboard. She's a bit nervous about Grace's decision not to carry parachutes. Still, it's her show and Willa didn't question out loud any of the decisions about what could and couldn't come with them on the flight. She has memorized the list of what she's permitted to bring. One pair of overalls, two long-sleeved white shirts, one pair of jodhpurs, a scarf, coat, helmet, two pairs of goggles (one tinted, one not), gloves, minimal underwear and socks, boots. She is also allowed oilskins in case of rain. Except for a toothbrush and face cream for the sun, that's it for personal belongings. The Moth has been rigged out with canvas hoods that lie flat against the fuselage when not in use and can be pulled up and over the heads of the pilots in inclement weather. All that protects them otherwise from the elements is the small nose-high windscreen in front of each cockpit.

The endurance flight will be made or broken on the success of the food and fuel drops. Another pilot from the Air Harbour will go aloft with Jack Robson in the refuelling plane and drop the bag containing supplies, food and water attached to the fuel hose. This will be the most dangerous part of the flight. The tank is on top of the centre section of the upper wing, right over the forward cockpit, so it will be Grace who will have to grapple with securing the refuelling hose. It will require steady formation flying on the part of Willa and Jack to keep it all under control.

Jack.

Willa soaps her toes. She can't imagine what he must be feeling. She bets it's not pleasant. She hasn't had many dealings with Jack Robson, but she's liked what little she knows of him. Steady worker. Patient instructor. Dependable. Well, she hopes he remains dependable for this flight. The situation unsettles her. It can't be without emotion and that's where problems always develop, in the shifting space between emotion and action.

Grace.

It is still hard to believe that Grace O'Gorman, heroine of the skies, has asked Willa to help her break a record. Willa has never even dared dream of meeting Grace, let alone to be flying with her for twenty-five days as her only companion. It is both terrifying and exhilarating. A dream she was afraid to have that has come true anyway.

After her bath Willa tidies her cabin a little, puts books back on shelves, takes clothes from the floor and folds them neatly back into drawers. She heats up some soup, eats it out of the saucepan, standing in front of the window, watching the sun roll its bulk down behind the islands. What will it mean to live in the sky? What will it be like to circle and circle this one patch of familiar ground?

For endurance flights to be legitimate they must take off and land at the same place and be obviously visible for the duration of the attempt. For that reason all endurance flights are circular events. They are also required to carry a barograph, an instrument that detects any improper landings by recording fluctuations in atmospheric pressure. Without it the flight will not be officially recognized and the resulting aviation record cannot be noted.

They'll have to be careful about their altitude. A recent attempt in California had the area residents complaining about the noise of the plane as it spun on its axis over their houses. Fifteen hundred feet or higher, thinks Willa, sucking broth off her spoon. The height at which it's hard to distinguish people. Buildings are visible, and trees, but the shape and motion of the human body don't really exist at fifteen hundred feet. No people. Another thing to be missed. Just Grace for company and no real talking because the noise will be too severe. They'll have to write notes. Grace hasn't allowed a speaking tube in her mania for keeping the weight down. No speaking tube. No parachutes.

It suddenly occurs to Willa that she has no idea what Grace O'Gorman is really like, beyond what's common knowledge of the famous aviatrix. What if she doesn't like her? What if she gets up there, at an altitude where human life on the ground is invisible, and the only companion she has is a big disappointment?

Willa shivers even though it's not the least bit cold in her cabin. She starts to anticipate her loneliness. She's suddenly aware of exactly what it is she is doing. She's putting herself in exile, high up there in the empty, darkened sky.

She is leaving earth.

A T 6:00 on the morning of Tuesday, August 1, 1933, the overloaded Moth DH60T, with Grace O'Gorman at the controls, rises shakily into an overcast sky. There is a small group of well-wishers to see them off, a smattering of clapping as the plane teeters at the edge of the runway and reluctantly slopes up over the waves.

There had been the requisite newspaper photographs with Willa and Grace standing in their overalls beside the *Adventure Girl* logo. Willa and Grace waving from the cockpits of the stationary Moth, all smiles. Grace with fresh lipstick. Deep red. A reporter even asking her the colour. She laughs and jokes with him. "Forever Airborne," she says.

Willa and Grace have opted to circle the Toronto harbour anti-clockwise. Airplane propellers always rotate in one direction and that bias makes a plane pull either to the left or to the right. By flying anti-clockwise they will be following the natural inclination of the Moth to lean into the left.

Once up in the sky there is almost a scramble to establish routine. Grace levels off at fifteen hundred feet and eighty miles per hour, starts a slow left bank over the eastern side of the bay. Willa writes in the logbook their exact time of departure and the schedule for the day — three-hour flying rotations, refuelling every eight hours. She also begins timing their first full loop of city, C.N.E., islands, lake, industrial port lands, city. Ten minutes. For a brief moment she considers calculating how many loops they will fly in twenty-five days, but manages to restrain herself. It would be too overwhelming to know this.

It is not the best day to begin their endeavour. The air is thick with humidity. The temperature is already up into the eighties, with a predicted high for the day of over one hundred degrees. There is a gusty wind bubbling along below one thousand feet. The waves in the bay topple white. It smells like rain.

With Grace doing the first flying shift, Willa gets a chance to establish herself in her surroundings. She sits in a cockpit separated from the one in front by a ten-inch strip of metal fuselage. Grace is close enough for Willa to grab by the shoulder or kick under the seat. She rests her arms on the sides of the cockpit and feels the wash from the propeller buffet her shoulders and the top of her head where it's not protected by windscreen. This is how fatigue happens, the muscles in the body always tensed against the force of the slipstream, no way to escape the pressure.

From the waist up, Willa's cockpit is roomy enough. She can touch the fuselage walls with bent elbows but there's space out in the open air to stretch her arms. She raises herself up by gripping the sides of the plane, pushing down. She rises up off the padded metal seat as far as her safety harness will allow, lets herself drop back down again.

In front of Willa is the flight panel with its gauges in a half-moon across the face — oil temperature, tachometer, altimeter, airspeed indicator, oil pressure. The throttle is a lever on the left side of the fuselage, above the trim knob. A compass is mounted ahead of the control column on the floor. Between her legs is the stick. Both legs stretch forward in separate chambers under the control panel to operate the rudder pedals.

Willa experiments with different sitting positions. Knees pulled up so her feet sit squarely either side of the stick. Both legs drawn up on the same side of the stick, body angled across the cockpit, twisting in the harness and leaning hard against the side wall. She undoes her harness. Stands up. The rush of one-hundred-mile-an-hour air hauls the breath out of her, wobbles her body. Her goggles push against her eyes, the chinstrap from her cloth helmet bounces on her neck. She raises her arms straight out at her sides and gets promptly knocked back into her seat.

Grace, seemingly unaware of Willa's movements behind her, brings the plane over the city.

Willa buckles her harness on again, looks down. Being in the rear cockpit she has the best view of the ground. The forward cockpit is simply a nest between the wings.

From the air the city is all shape. Horseshoe of the roundhouse train station. Piano keys of ferry and steamship docks. Flat dinner plate of Maple Leaf baseball stadium. Straws of chimneys from the factories and refineries. Buildings as squares or oblongs, the steel roofs of dockyard warehouses glinting like metal teeth in a jaw of concrete. Rail tracks like stitches, sewn sloppily across the bottom end of the city.

There's a high whine above the engine and wind noise. Air whips around the rigging: the truss from which wires or stays form a number of triangles that bind the wings to each other and to the body of the plane.

Willa grabs her pencil and pad of paper from its pocket under the dashboard. Passes the note to Grace.

Okay?

Grace makes the previously decided signal for Willa to take the stick: one arm straight up in the air.

Willa eases the plane over the islands and Grace hands back the piece of paper.

Isn't it all so small.

Adventure Girl's first in-air refuelling is successful. Just after two o'clock a plane rises up from the Air Harbour and falls into stride with the Moth. They fly for a few moments, testing the balance, stacked and banking in tandem. A canvas bag and length of rubber hose drop from the open door of the mono-plane. Jack keeps the refuelling plane steady. Willa keeps the Moth steady. Grace flails through the air, snags the drifting cargo, hauls it in. She unties the bag and manoeuvres it into her cockpit, secures the rope that held the bag onto a metal eye on the band of fuselage between the cockpits. Standing up she undoes the fuel tank, lets the metal cap flap on the end of its chain and slides the hose into the empty clang of the tank.

The Moth has been fitted out with a forty-gallon tank in the upper wing where there would usually be a twenty. There are also three portable four-gallon tins of fuel that are wedged into the sides of the front cockpit which Grace can pump up into the main tank using a hand pump, when the main tank is almost empty. The hand pump is also used to deliver oil, through a permanent feeder tube, to the oil compartment at the base of the engine. Depending on the Moth's airspeed and the wind and weather, the fifty-two gallons of fuel give Grace and Willa between eight and nine hours of flight. To be on the safe side they have arranged with Jack to come and refuel them every eight hours.

When full, the tank of fuel weighs almost five hundred pounds and Willa is careful to pull back a little on the stick, keeping the nose up as the increasing heaviness flattens the buoyancy the Moth enjoyed when empty.

They fly over the eastern gap and down over the black hills of coal in the port lands.

Grace replaces the fuel cap and waves with her hand for the refuelling plane to pull in the hose. As the nozzle clears the upper wings she undoes the canvas bag and dumps out the contents — three full tins of fuel and a cloth-wrapped food package. She piles the empty tins into the bag, stows the full ones along the sides of her cockpit, signals for the bag to be raised.

The monoplane releases itself from the orbit of the Moth and jags sharply down towards the city.

Willa looks at her watch. The whole refuelling episode took less than fifteen minutes.

Grace is busy tying the fuel tins against the fuselage. She stood for most of the refuelling and Willa knows the strength it takes to balance and brace against the slipstream. What will they do when they've been up here for a while and their bodies are tired and weak? Grace will have to tie herself onto the plane somehow. Willa thinks of her parachute, square and compact, sitting on the floor beside her bed, at home.

Grace, kneeling backwards in her seat, struggling with the food package and trying to keep her feet out of the way of the stick, looks up suddenly at Willa and smiles. She's removed her goggles for the refuelling and there are marks from them rimming her eyes like shadows. Her recently reapplied lipstick glows red.

Willa smiles back. She is surprised at how emotional she feels, realizes how isolated she was with only Grace's helmet to look at, the shoulders of her overalls. And Grace has only the exposed cylinders, the exhaust pipe, the wires of the engine to gaze out over. She must be glad to see me too, thinks Willa. They are tossed up in the air, a shiny bouquet, and what they have now is each other. Willa looks at Grace and, for the first time, thinks of her not as a magazine photo or a newspaper headline but as someone who is *like* Willa. Someone who is within reach.

Nice to see you, she scrawls, the paper held awkwardly against her thigh with her wrist as she writes with one hand and steers with the other.

You too.

The heat doesn't dissipate with twilight. With the aid of their altitude Willa and Grace have managed to shed about five degrees, but the temperature, according to Willa's small thermometer, is still swelling towards one hundred.

They have eaten cheese sandwiches and apples, tossed the cores into the water off the northern shore of the islands. Willa has peed into the white enamel chamber pot, shaking it briskly over the side, swilling it out with disinfectant. Peeing is difficult wearing overalls and Willa decides to change her clothes tomorrow into the more functional shirt and jodhpurs.

It's five o'clock. They have been airborne for eleven hours and already Willa feels numb with fatigue. She drops five hundred feet and extends the loop, for variety. Flies over the two-masted schooner *Lyman M. Davis*, moored out from Sunnyside Beach and awaiting its demise as a bonfire on the August long weekend. It's the last of the Great Lakes schooners, over eighty feet long with a bowsprit tacking its prow to the horizon. Willa doesn't hold with the public's enthusiasm for torching old boats. From one thousand feet up there doesn't seem to be anything wrong with the *Lyman M. Davis*. Why not let it keep sailing? Willa believes that ships and planes carry the faintest traces of those who sailed or flew in them. Memory brushed into the hulls, the sails and wings. A part of everyone who ever touched the rails or worked the ropes. That should be respected, not incinerated as a holiday amusement.

Willa has loosened the loop of the Moth and dropped its ceiling partially to see if she'll be able to watch any of the women's baseball game that starts at 8:00 at Sunnyside. Her favourite team, the Supremes, will be pitching against the Lakesides. She has friends on the Supremes. From her perch in the air she can see the large, ornate stone Sunnyside Bathing Pavilion, the remains of the hydro tower, the perfect symmetry of the baseball diamond. Willa writes a note to Grace, whose turn it is to fly when the game begins.

Baseball? Supremes are playing. Keep us low.

They never get a chance to watch the ball game. By eight o'clock the sky is blistered with clouds. The wind at a thousand feet is minimal but, down below the water peaks, stiffens white. In ten-minute intervals as they near, fly over and leave a section of seawall at what looks to be the foot of Bathurst Street, they see a large sailing boat crunch and churn against the concrete. When Grace drops lower they can see people clinging to the rigging, thrashing like tiny dolls as the boat starts to drop its stern down into the water, begins to sink.

There's a child up the mast.

MIRO, KING OF ALL FAT BABIES, sits naked in his small bathtub, water to his waist.

Maddy, balanced on the edge of the porcelain, soaps him roughly. She surfs the bar along his rollers of fat, sometimes inserting it into a fold, pinching the skin shut over it so that the bar of soap shoots along the hidden channel and pops out under an armpit.

"Not so hard," says Miro, when Maddy pushes down against the back of his neck as if she's trying to erase it.

Maddy ignores him. "You're a baby," she says finally. "You can't complain."

Miro is not really a baby. He's a twenty-seven-year-old dwarf who sits propped up in a display case at the front of his tiny house every day from noon to midnight, dressed in diapers and holding a rattle. People can tap on the glass and he'll roll around a bit to show how fat he is and how difficult it is to move. That part is true. It is difficult for Miro to move around, and twice a week he pays Maddy ten cents to wash him. A private arrangement. *Don't tell your parents. Just in case.*

Maddy quite likes washing Miro. She's a lot bigger than he is and this gives her the confidence of a bully. She likes his fat body. Sometimes she'll experiment with different washing agents. Once she rubbed him all over with weeds from the lake, draping them decoratively around his neck as though he were a fat piece of flotsam. Once she painted on his back with mud. Flexible as she is about the materials, Maddy has strict rules about other parts of the ritual. She gets to listen to the radiogram afterwards, and for as long as she wants. She gets paid promptly after each bath, and with a dime, not two nickels or ten pennies. And she won't wash the King of All Fat Babies between the legs, no matter how helplessly he asks. "Wash that yourself," she says. "It's ugly, I'm not touching it." If he makes too much of a fuss, she slaps him until he shuts up.

Today Maddy is taking no pleasure in Miro's fleshy cascade. She is anxious to finish the bath and be allowed to listen to the radio. She needs to know how the pilots survived their first night. She had lain in bed, for so long awake, ears straining for the high-up rattle of engine. On her wall, near her pillow, is a colour picture of Grace O'Gorman cut from a magazine.

"You're hurting me," complains Miro, his hand suddenly grabbing her wrist as she soaps his chest. "Stop it."

He's surprisingly strong today, but even so Maddy twists easily away. "I'm finished anyway," she says and, picking up the saucepan from the floor, ladles water over him.

"Help me out then," says Miro. "Nicely."

Maddy hauls him to his feet, leaning backwards for balance and pulling his soft arms up.

"Don't." Miro seems about to cry.

Maddy rubs him with a towel, gently. She doesn't want him to burst into tears and make a fuss. Nothing must get in her way of listening to the radiogram. "If you're good," she says, "I'll rub some powder on you."

Miro sits in his special miniature armchair next to the wooden case of the radiogram. Maddy stands behind him, dumping a fine rain of baby powder onto his shoulders and back and absent-mindedly patting at it as it pools on his lumpy skin.

The radio crackles as the tubes warm up. Spit of electricity down the wires.

The cloud of baby powder is making it hard to breathe. Miro has begun to choke, his whole body wobbling. Maddy puts the container of powder down on top of the radiogram. "Don't cough," she says, and suddenly feeling friendly towards him she bends over and fiercely kisses the top of his shaved head.

The radio news, unbelievably, begins with other things. More statistics of people out of work and on relief. The sinking of a yawl last night by the seawall and the subsequent rescue of those aboard — seven men, five women and a child, pulled from the wreckage. More record heat-wave temperatures. Finally, near the very end of the broadcast, when Maddy is so agitated that she is stamping up and down, there is news about her precious pilots. Circling and doing fine after completing their first day of in-air refuelling. Seem to be in high spirits.

"How dull," says Miro. "Chasing their tail for twenty-five days."

Maddy leans over him, her face upside down and right in front of his. "They can see you," she says. "They look down from the sky and they know who you are. They know that you've been bad."

Miro sighs. "Oh, Christ," he says. "Turn to something with singing."

THE SECOND DAY in the air feels altogether different from the first. For one thing it's a lot cooler, only sixty-eight degrees at 8:00 A.M. when the previous day it had been eighty degrees by the same time. Willa and Grace wear their leather flight jackets and gloves against the early-morning chill as they bank slow over the misted lake, everything still below them.

It's as if no one's down there, writes Willa, first in the logbook and then on a piece of paper passed over to Grace.

Willa hunches into the warmth of her jacket, drinks the last of her thermos of coffee from the 6:00 A.M. refuelling/food drop. She feels a bit stiff, but otherwise not as bad as she'd expected. They haven't had a lot of rest, their bodies not yet used to the three-hour rotations and refusing to be instantly cooperative and sleep soundly in small allotments.

Willa thinks about the sinking yacht as they fly over the seawall, the water clouded white with fog. They'd had to climb to escape the wind last night and hadn't seen what had happened to the people aboard. Grace had sent Jack a note this morning asking about it, so maybe they'd have an answer at 2:00.

Willa is grateful for the daylight, and for a day of blue sky and sun. Flying at night, with only the two small lights on their wing-tips and the silver splash of moon, was an isolating experience. There were times, when the moon was behind the clouds or when they'd risen too high above the greasy residue of city lights, that Willa could barely see the shape of Grace in the forward cockpit. They hung flashlights around their necks to read the instruments and write each other notes. Willa digs in her jacket pocket, reads some of the things Grace said to her last night.

Keep us steady, I need to pump oil in.

Sleep an extra hour if you want. I'm okay.

The moon's a crazy sweetheart.

Willa smiles. She likes that one. Passed over to her at 4:00 A.M. when the moonlight skidded in manic zigzags across the tops of the waves.

The Moth has behaved admirably in its first twenty-four hours of non-stop flying. The steady bark of the engine is now a rhythm pressed into Willa's nerves and bones. They haven't burned as much oil as they'd expected and the pump system has worked fine for the transfer of both fuel and oil to their respective tanks. Grace's mechanic, Alex, has done such a good job adjusting the rigging wires that the stick can be worked with fingertips. Even the right-rudder correction, endemic to left-leaning Moths, is minimal because of the anti-clockwise direction of the flight. The only thing that they still have trouble with is the difference in handling the plane when it is fully loaded with fuel and when it is empty. The Moth was not made to carry as much fuel weight as they've forced upon it and consequently the extra twenty gallons on the upper wings make it awkwardly top-heavy. They have to be careful that banking the fully loaded plane is done gradually. No steep angles that could flip them over onto their back. Willa is glad that it's Grace who usually flies the Moth right after refuelling. She likes the plane best when it's nearly empty, when it springs and lifts like a helium balloon.

The sun is starting to enter the plane. Willa reaches behind her into the fuselage compartment where she keeps her belongings. She needs to change her goggles to the tinted ones and to put some cream on her face. Yesterday she got sunburned — looking in the small mirror that they have ostensibly for emergency signalling and actually for Grace to use when applying fresh lipstick, she had been alarmed at the redness of her skin. They have to be wary of the sun on days like today when the sky is so clear, an upside-down blue bowl curving over the flat of earth.

Willa takes off her gloves, smooths the cream liberally over her face and then passes the jar forward. Grace has her own supply, stashed up with her belongings in a storage compartment in front of her, but it's easier for her to dip her fingers into the jar as Willa holds it.

Grace nods when she's finished applying the cream and Willa caps the jar, shoves it back into the innards of her pack. She stretches her arms up, feels the sun pool on her jacket. She's surprised at how good she feels. A lightness. A rising bubble of happiness. This is as long as she's ever been in the air continuously and her feeling for flying seems to have expanded in the last twenty-four hours beyond any expectation she ever had for her vocation. This is what she was born to do, it's as easy as that.

I love this.

And Grace writes back.

That's because you're a natural.

What is that, Willa wonders. She knows she feels most herself when she's in a plane. She knows then that she *is* flight, that it works through her body as a sense like sight or touch. It throws her forward, makes her burn, all nerves and adrenaline, the hot twist of her heart in a fuselage of ribs.

If that is what it is to be a natural, to be a flyer, then what is Grace O'Gorman, who handles a plane so finely that her skill invades the minds of those watching and makes everything — the perfect pitch of the day, their own lives — seem incomplete?

What do you call yourself? Willa slips the note to Grace over her shoulder, brushes the stiff skin of her jacket, the rising heat.

I don't.

Willa slides back, leans her head against the padded strip of leather on the rear of the cockpit. She can see the loose strands of Grace's red hair hooking the air at the nape of her neck. She can see the sun run a smooth finger of light along the trailing edge of the upper wings.

Grace's hand snaps backwards, a piece of paper outstretched to Willa.

You name me.

WHAT WILLA NOTICES the most on her second day in the air is the colour of the world below the plane. The black stacks of coal in the port lands, a small mountain range of a shade so dark that it begins to fall out of the colour around it, the lake and land, and become the opposite of what it is — a hole that collapses blackness into blackness. A hollow for the eye to fall into.

The city, when Willa avoids picking out familiar buildings and landmarks, looks like a scattering of loose multicoloured bricks, piled up on dark rectangles of bare earth. Rubble, the city looks like rubble, like something knocked down.

Roads flicker like rivers in the changing light.

Smoke unravels in vowels from pencil-stub factory chimneys.

The islands, in their half-circle, their *C* curve, hold the shape of the bay. Trees mass green. Lagoons and ponds are dramatically cut out from the land. There is the flesh of beach where the skin of grass and trees has peeled back.

Roofs of island houses, small coloured beads.

Masts of boats in the yacht club basin, stiff and spiny like the bristles of a brush. The metallic zipper flash of the amusement park as they fly over Hanlan's Point.

And so many colours of green.

But it is the water that Willa can't get over. The infinite gradations of shading, notching the colour blue a little this way towards grey, a little that way towards green. The lighter aureole around the deeper dark of land. The coils of shade under the water, old piers or the bones of sunken boats. The deep, deep of the middle of the lake, layers of blue piled up from a place so far down that it glows dimly as if somewhere under the water there's a light left on; a sunken star.

———

Just before two o'clock Willa brings the Moth lower, looks for the refuelling plane leaving the ground. They fly over the city side. Willa reads the words *Air Harbour* painted on the roof of the hangar, spots a monoplane taxiing towards the lake.

The transfer of fuel goes smoothly enough. Grace, getting more adept at handling the hose, finishes the exchange quicker than usual. The empty tins are hoisted up, the full ones are stowed safely away. There's a package of food and a newspaper. No reply from Jack to Grace's letter. Grace waves at the plane but no one responds. The gas hose winds in. The refuelling plane drops out of sight beneath them.

Willa begins a climb to combat the heaviness of the overloaded Moth. Grace, food bundle unopened on her lap, is reading the front page of the newspaper. She twists around in her seat, holds the paper flat across the metal between the cockpits so that Willa can read what she's pointing to, a picture of the Moth circling out over the islands.

"Girl Flyers Make It Through First Night Aloft."

There's a story below it. Willa keeps the plane level, reads the text. "'We're tired and bored,' says Willa Briggs, one of the daring lady pilots, in a note sent yesterday to Jack Robson in the refuelling plane. 'But we're determined to keep going.'"

That's as far as Willa gets. Grace has snatched the paper away before she can continue reading more quotes of things she never said. Her body goes suddenly cold. What is going on? The only note sent to Jack was the one from Grace at 6:00 this morning, asking about the fate of the sinking boat. Nothing from Willa. Nothing at all.

Grace swivels in her seat, her blue eyes bright with rage, unfolds a piece of paper for Willa to read.

That bastard.

MADDY LIES IN BED in her small upstairs room, listening to her parents and Simon talk down below in the kitchen. The downstairs light has crept up the staircase and stretches sallow across the wall by her head. She lifts and lowers an arm, making the shadow of a wing as she hears the thin buzz of Grace O'Gorman's plane pass overhead.

In the cramped kitchen Fram and Del sit at the wooden table. Simon paces between the sink and the back door, reading from the front page of a newspaper that he clutches in one hand. "'God Calls Kill Off the Jews, Nazis Openly Call for Pogrom . . . Jews are not humans, it is proclaimed, but poisonous snakes . . .'" Simon smacks *Der Yiddisher Zhurnal* down on the counter and jams his hands in his pant pockets. "That's what's happening over there with the new Chancellor Hitler. Self-appointed man of the people. Jewish businesses shut down. Doctors not allowed to practise. Books by Jews fodder for bonfires. And now . . ." Simon leans back against the sink. "Now we have the Swastika Club in Toronto painting swastikas on the canoe club building and walking up and down the boardwalk — whole gangs of them — in their blue shirts and pants, wearing that stupid chrome swastika badge. 'Help get rid of the Jews. Keep the beaches clean.'" He rocks back against the sink, arms crossed over his chest, sweat dampening the loose hair hanging over his forehead.

Del at the table pours herself and Fram more tea, rubs a hand carefully over the back of her neck. "It's not just the beaches, Simon," she says. She looks right at her brother, thinks of how familiar he is to her, that lean face, the way his body notches against the counter. More known to her in some ways than her husband of fourteen years. She can't remember a time before Simon.

"It happens here. No Jews allowed to live or tent on Ward's Island. All those Gentiles Only signs outside the fancy hotels and the yacht club. But it's benign compared to Europe. Ma had a letter from the uncles. They're trying to leave." Del lowers her hand from her neck to the mug of tea in front of her. "There's talk that people are being detained for no reason. Locked up."

"Bloody hell," says Fram, sputtering over his tea. "Benign! Del, do you think Fatty Bennett's returning policy is harmless? Sending those in the relief camps back where they come from, shipping Jews back to Europe. To Germany. To Hitler." Fram lowers his voice, but upstairs in her room Maddy hears him clear as if he were standing by her bed. "Will it end at arresting Jews?" he says, looking from his wife to his brother-in-law. "Boycotting Jewish businesses? Stopping Jews from marrying non-Jews? People are leaving because they fear there's worse to come."

Maddy presses her face against the picture of Grace O'Gorman on her wall. Her hot cheek against Grace's cool, cool paper skin. She waits for the noise of the Moth over the voice of her father, but it's too distant yet to hear. Maddy closes her eyes, pushes hard into the shiny, smooth lips of the famous aviatrix. "You mustn't wait," she whispers. "I haven't long."

B Y THE THIRD NIGHT Willa has lost all feelings of euphoria for the flight. They have been replaced by the more practical concerns of discomfort. The weather has turned colder. Only sixty-eight degrees in the middle of the day and low sixties now that night is coming on. Grey clouds swell the horizon shut.

All of Willa's body has stiffened in sympathy with the cold. Even though she wears a jacket, scarf and gloves over her shirt and jodhpurs, her arms are heavy and slow. Every day she has tried to exercise, remembering what Simon Kahane said about being loose, but today the side-to-side punches and the leg lifts don't help at all. It's not the cold she's fighting — it's everything.

Each circle that they fly over the harbour adds another layer to Willa's unease. She's cold and tired, only managing to sleep soundly through Grace's midnight to 3:00 A.M. shift. She wants to stretch her legs, eat a hot meal. She wants a bath. She washes her face and neck every day with the rubbing alcohol because they get so filthy from the engine backdraft, and yesterday she even swatted at her armpits and between her breasts. But it is not really *washing*. Willa wants her tub — hot water, her legs draping langorously over the porcelain stem.

The smallest rituals are an ordeal. Even brushing her teeth is a complication. First there's the rummage through the rear compartment for her brush and the toothpaste. Baiting the brush is easy enough, thrashing around the inside of her mouth. She swills with water from the flask that she keeps beside her seat. To spit Willa has to haul herself half over the side of the plane so that the toothpaste drool drops away from the fuselage and not straight back into her hair as happened on the first day when she just stuck her head over the side and opened her mouth. If Grace is unaware of what Willa is doing (which she often is when she's flying) and chooses the moment when Willa is hanging upside down to spit as the moment to steepen the bank of the Moth, Willa is in danger of being catapulted from her cockpit with a mouth full of mint-flavoured toothpaste.

She wants out of the plane.

She's sore from sitting so much. She's constipated and has a backache. Her legs get numb when she's working the rudder pedals. The noise of the engine, like a swarm of bees inside her head, is making it hard to think.

Both Grace and Willa have stopped wearing their safety harnesses. Safety harnesses were a fine idea if all you were doing was flying, but they are a complete nuisance when it comes to refuelling or peeing or changing clothes or brushing teeth.

And now, just after 8:00 P.M. on Thursday, August 3, it starts to rain. Grace is flying the last hour of her evening rotation. The sun set twenty minutes ago but the clouds still hold a glow, enough to see by.

At the feel of the first few drops against her face Willa twists in her seat, unfastens the canvas hood from the fuselage and unfolds it up and over her head. The canvas is ribbed with half-circles of bamboo, the ends of which drop into small metal cups attached at eight-inch intervals to the outside of the doors. The front of the canvas doesn't come down as far as the windscreen, there's a gap of about a foot through which the slipstream bounds in and tries to rip the flimsy hood right off. Willa holds onto the front of the canvas with one hand and with the other grabs Grace by the shoulder, trying to signal to her to raise her hood while Willa flies the plane.

The hoods, especially designed for them by an *Adventure Girl* staffer, don't work very well. Because the plane is moving forward at seventy miles an hour the rain drives in at an angle through the space above the windscreen and in minutes Willa is soaked. Trying to get to her oilskins she briefly lets go of the canvas and it tears from the body of the plane and disappears behind her into the swirl of storm. Grace, who is a bit more sheltered up in the wings, has managed to hold onto hers with one hand while she continues to operate the stick with the other.

By the time Willa has struggled into her oilskins she's completely wet. Water runs from her sodden helmet down her neck and back. Her goggles are smeared with rain and she can't see anything. Only her feet, tucked into the rudder channels either side of Grace's seat, are still dry.

Willa rips off her goggles and her helmet, tosses them to the floor. She tries to squeeze her body down under the tiny windscreen but the stick gets in the way.

Thunder starts its rough rattle above the plane.

Lightning, thinks Willa. What if the Moth is pinned out by lightning? She kicks Grace's seat with her right foot, because she can't see Grace under the canvas bowl and she's starting to panic. Who's flying the plane? What if the engine gets too wet and cuts out, the sweet machine whine that Willa once cursed but now clings to with every nerve in her body.

A hand snakes through from underneath Grace's hood. Willa unpeels the piece of damp paper.

Yours.

My what? thinks Willa. Rain rocks the little plane from side to side, streams off the trailing edge of the upper wing in a veil. The Moth goes into a port stall. It takes a moment for Willa to realize that no one's flying the plane.

———

The 10:00 P.M. refuelling is a disaster. The monoplane can't lock its orbit with the Moth. Grace's canvas hood blows off as she's trying to grab the hose, which keeps jerking out of reach as the refuelling plane corrects and recorrects its position. When she finally does manage to hold onto it with both hands, she is lifted partially out of the cockpit as the other plane rises. Willa thinks that Jack is trying to steal Grace and shoves the nose of the Moth up abruptly so that Grace drops back into the cockpit.

The tank-filling doesn't go well. The two planes can't seem to pace the sky together and twice the hose is yanked from the filler cap, spraying gasoline over Grace and the front cockpit. Willa, who can barely see to fly, has to try to keep the plane perfectly smooth and level while Grace frantically paws at the swinging hose. The wing tank never gets completely filled and Willa hopes that Jack will check his levels when he gets back to the Air Harbour, will notice that it wasn't a total fill and will come back appropriately early for the next refuelling.

There is no note from Jack, no words from above. Grace stows the fuel tins and undoes the food parcel to find only a thermos of soup, some biscuits, some dried dates. She kneels backwards on her seat, unscrews the thermos lid. Grace is totally sodden. She never had time to put on her oilskins. Her clothes stick to her body. The helmet plastered to her scalp makes her look bald.

Lightning trembles the night sky, the clouds. Willa flies the plane and Grace feeds her hot tomato soup as they glide in their groove over the city, over the water, over the islands. Willa with her mouth open, the thick soup on her tongue as warm and salty as blood. The smell of gasoline from Grace's skin.

The storm has finally blown off by the 5:09 sunrise. Willa sees it leave, scudding west down the sky, gusting itself farther along the shore. The constant shift of the heavens, she thinks. Moving weather in and out on a whim, flashing day/night/day, moon, no moon. Shiny tin punctures of stars.

Grace sleeps under her oilskins, her head vibrating softly against the fuselage. She's removed her helmet and Willa watches her red hair dry slowly in the returning sun. The relief of morning and the rain ending has made Willa calmer. She moves the stick with her fingertips, barely touching the leather-wrapped steel. She watches the sun come up. She watches Grace sleep.

It is not until half an hour later, when Willa spots the refuelling plane scuttling across the tarmac below and she's looking for a piece of paper and pencil to write Jack a reprimand for his invented quotations, that she discovers the true damage from last night's storm.

Paper.

The notepads, the logbook, the newspaper — all ruined, all soggy gelatinous masses. The pencils simply gone, flushed out of the plane with all the rain and motion, or back into the tail where they can't be reached. Unknown to Willa and Grace the rainwater has been sluicing around in the bilge of the fuselage, running back into Willa's belongings when the plane nosed up, forward into Grace's when the plane nosed down. Everything is wet, but everything can be dried, except for the paper. It is perhaps the most essential piece of equipment that they have. Willa has become used to not speaking, to talking to Grace on paper.

The monoplane spirals up to meet them. Grace sleeps in the forward cockpit, her head twisted on its side, cheek against the metal strip that separates the cockpits, her eyes closed. Willa continues her search for dry paper, for a lucky, saved pencil.

How can I reach you now?

"HOLD YOUR REINS in your left hand," says Fram. "No slack."
This morning Maddy is learning how to mount her black carousel horse correctly. Left foot hooked up in the stirrup, she bounces down on her right, hands clawing for the saddle horn.

"Did you check the cinch?" asks Fram from the other side of the horse. "You wouldn't want it to be slipping now, would you?"

Maddy scowls at him. Her legs hurt. "Dad. It's glued on."

"Well, yes, I know." Fram puts a hand on the worn leather saddle, pats it gently.

It's cool this morning. There's a wind from the lake that swirls a chill around the inside of the carousel.

Fram sighs, his breath limp in the stiff air. "Look, girl, it's like this." He swings astride the horse that's in front of his daughter's, one easy motion from the ground to the saddle.

While he's sitting in his demonstrated perfect riding stance Maddy manages to drag herself up the side of the black horse on her belly and swivel into a sitting position. "Dad?" says Maddy, because he's just so still, not saying anything and looking out over the lake. He's as solid and rigid as the chestnut he rides.

Fram drops down off his horse, turns on the carousel. "Let's have a go, shall we?" He remounts on the run, his horse bobbing up and down fast in its circle with him trotting beside it for a while and then launching himself from ground to stirrup to saddle, almost gracefully. Just a little stumble, a little hesitation.

"I'm galloping across the heather and you're there too . . ." begins Maddy, but her father holds up his hand and she stops her story. She can't see his face at all and she can't tell what he's thinking from his straight back, but she does as he wants. They ride the painted horses in silence around and around the track. Out over the water, back over the land. There's the machine noise and the high gasp of the wind as it tears by them. There's the metallic smell of dead fish, weeds.

Once her father squeezes his legs into the horse's flanks as though this will break the orbit, will send the brown horse on a canter across the amusement park and out onto the green grass fields of Hanlan's Point. For all that he's told her about being a boy in Scotland, riding rough all day on the moors, Maddy can't imagine it. What she can see instead is this man, her father, as he is now, silently riding that painted lifeless horse along the beach of the western bar. Sitting all stiff like that, rising up and down in the saddle in even, measured beats.

A wooden horse would make a nice sound on the board-walk, she thinks. A wooden horse would float. She imagines them floating away on their horses, out into the middle of the lake. Just the two of them. They could land on some empty island, build a little house out of sticks. They would have fish for dinner and lunch and breakfast. Maddy is not that fond of fish, but she would learn to like it, she *could* learn to like it. It would be good to be away with her father, away from her mother and the thing she is that nobody likes. The thing she is that Maddy refuses to become. The taunts every day from the Bell twins, all the way home from school this spring. *Jew-girl. Dirty little Jew-girl.*

Maddy rides behind her father, holds the reins firmly but not too tight. Just like he taught her.

MADDY RIDES her bicycle down the Blockhouse Bay side of Hanlan's Point. Hanlan's is a peninsula — on the western side is the boat regatta course and the western sandbar, on the eastern side of the point is Blockhouse Bay, a narrow stretch of water running between Hanlan's and Mugg's Island. Near the bottom of the bay, where it spreads tendrils around the base of Mugg's and some smaller unnamed islands, there's the wreck of an old wooden barge. It lies close to the shore, decks resting on a sandbar, wheelhouse tilting its chin down towards the water.

Maddy dumps her bike behind some bushes, scrunches her pant legs up and wades out to the barge. The hull has completely rotted away and what's left of it is silted over. She scrambles up the side, using the broken boards as footholds and stands on the slanted deck of the boat. There is no shortage of wrecked boats around the islands. Mostly they are burned as weekend entertainment in the summer, but the barge that Maddy stands on has been left too long for that. It's sunk far into the sand, and the few boards of the wheelhouse and deck would make a disappointing bonfire.

Maddy pushes open the crooked door of the wheelhouse,

hanging on one hinge, the words *Keep Out* painted on in white. Inside there's a tall chair in front of a dashboard, a gear-shift lever on the floor, a bare board where there used to be a bunk. (Maddy threw out the foam bunk cushion because it was full of mice nests.) There are some old fuel and tobacco tins on the floor, and some glass from the several broken windows. The one intact window is above the dashboard. Maddy pulls herself up into the chair and looks out up the bay towards the open water of the harbour. The barge ran aground and sank when it was going out from the islands, when it was on its way somewhere. She flicks a switch on the control panel, checks her gauges.

"It's flying like a bird, Grace," she says.

She kicks at the gear lever with both feet and manages to shift it a click forward. "I've let the power in," she says. "We can go higher."

There's a sudden bump at the back of the barge and voices. Boys' voices.

"Just an old wreck."

"Come on."

Another bump and then the scrabble of people climbing up the hull.

Maddy drops out of her chair, quickly pushes the door shut and braces herself hard against it.

Someone shoves it.

"Locked."

Someone tries again, this time with more force. Maddy drives her back against the thin piece of wood, heels grinding down into the wheelhouse floor. The door bends a little at the waist but holds.

"Nothing in there, anyway," says a voice. "Look. It's all just busted up."

Out of the corner of her eye Maddy can see two heads peering through the good dashboard window. Looking beyond where she's tucked back against the door. She doesn't move, holds her breath until she can hear them slipping down the side of the hull, their boat bumping as they get into it. When she's sure that they've gone, she crawls out of the wheelhouse, keeping low along the deck, to the stern of the barge.

Two boys in a canoe. Maddy recognizes the name on the boat — Sunfish Island Camp. The working boys' camp. Every August working city boys are given a holiday on Sunfish Island. Fishing, camping, boating, for young boys who haven't had much experience of leisure pursuits. Not that the camp is favoured by the islanders. The working boys have a reputation for wildness. Maddy has been warned away from them, as has every other child on the islands. There are lots of stories of things that the working boys have done. Drunk whisky and set fire to a bathing station. Shot cats with bows and arrows and then skinned them (and, in one rendition, eaten them). Set boats from the yacht club adrift on the lake. Whether the working boys have done these things or not, everyone agrees that they're entirely capable of doing them. It's just a matter of time.

Maddy watches the two boys disappear around Mugg's Island. She's breathing fast and flat, like a stone skidding quick across the water. "Gee, Grace," she says in a whisper. "We need to lock the plane."

Maddy rides her bicycle along the road on the northern shore of the main island. She's following the Moth. Every time it passes over her on its circuit she pedals as hard as she can, trying to stay beneath it for as long as possible, head down almost level with the handlebars, feet spinning the metal pedals, bike lurching from side to side with the sudden acceleration. The noise of the plane stirs the air around her. Birds whirl above the sand, above the driftwood barricade of beach.

While she waits for the Moth to loop back around to her again Maddy practises riding her bicycle in a circle with no hands, arms stuck out from her sides like the stiff broomstick wings of a scarecrow. It calms her down to imagine herself as the plane, up there in the safety of the empty sky, where nobody can get her.

MADDY SITS beside her father in the Mutual Street Arena. The place is full of men yelling insults and encouragement to the two eleven-year-old boys swinging at each other in the ring. Maddy sits eating from a bag of popcorn, looking more at the shouting crowd than the distant smoke-shrouded boys. Fram sits up straight in his chair beside her. He doesn't yell, has a clean shirt on, and his going-out-hair, all shiny and behaved.

Maddy isn't enamoured with the Mutual Street Arena. Her favourite boxing venue is the Palais Royale. All the fancy dancing people in their special clothes, throwing money at the fighters to egg them on. If you sit close enough to the ring, you can catch some of the change that comes bouncing off the canvas floor and through the ropes. Maddy once took home fifty cents from a Palais Royale night.

She even prefers the huge, new Maple Leaf Gardens to this grubby, smelly box of a room.

Made to come, she thinks grimly. Her mother working until midnight. No one to look after her. Why her parents worry so much about what happens at night is beyond her. She's alone all day and they don't seem concerned about that. It's the dark that makes them peel years from her age. Dark is just light turned inside out, thinks Maddy. Why be afraid of that?

"I could have stayed with Jim," she says. Jim is the man Fram asked to replace him for the evening at the merry-go-round. "I have before. Or Miro. Or Rose. Or Crocker." She lists off the people at the amusement park she has at one time or another been left with.

Fram glances at her absent-mindedly as if he's just remembered that she's there with him. "You like watching your uncle fight."

"I don't," says Maddy. "Maybe when I was ten." She thinks of the possible earnings if they were at the Palais Royale. "Maybe sometimes. But not," she says emphatically, "now."

Fram is not listening. He's sitting in his stiff way, watching as the boy in the blue trunks drives the boy in the white trunks against the spring of the ropes. The volume of the crowd surges as the white-trunked boy slides slowly sideways down to the mat and lies there without moving while the referee slaps the canvas by his head and counts him gone.

"Coward," says Maddy under her breath.

When she was interested in boxing — in the time before Grace O'Gorman flew into her heart and nested there — Simon would teach her the moves. She looks at the blue-trunked boy, all skinny ribs and bendy arms, and thinks that she could knock him out easy. A good left hook would flatten that floppy, sticking-up ear, and she has some powerful hook. She used to practise it against trees, her hands bandaged in rags. Maddy imagines the blue-trunked boy falling down, leaden as wood weight. Thunk against the forest floor.

Simon's fight is the last on the card. The main event. Kid Kahane against Slugger O'Brien. The Jew against the Mick. By the time they take to their corners the crowd is on their feet with rabid enthusiasm. Maddy sees the whole first round through the small triangles of space that men's bodies make when they're side by side.

Often Fram works Simon's corner, but tonight Simon has two of his friends from his street gang talk to him between rounds, wipe his face with a towel, suckle him water.

"Why's he hitting low all the time?" wonders Fram, hands on his knees and fishing his body this way and that to see between the men in front.

"Because Ma told him to," hisses Maddy.

When Simon had walked her home on Wednesday and made her some disgusting bean thing for supper he'd told her what Del had said about O'Brien. Soft. No rocks in the belly.

Fram looks anxiously over at Maddy. "I wish your mother would not do that."

Fram liked his wife's foretelling gifts to be used only for strangers, in the booth on Hanlan's Point. Twenty-five cents to tell an old woman that she'd soon find reason to travel or that her husband would recover from his illness. This is how it worked if you were a fortune-teller who had no real foresight, just a good imagination and keen perception. But Del truly had a flash of something that came from beyond the world of the amusement park. She'd told Maddy once that it was like seeing something move out of the corner of your eye, sometimes unrecognizable as a shape or form but you learned to respond to the gesture. Maddy had made her eyes sore by trying to walk around looking out of the corners of them. Del could predict events. She was unpleasantly adept at foretelling death. She was good at long shots. Simon's friends came to her to ask where to wager their money. She was good at telling Simon how to win his fights.

Maddy thought Del's advice to Simon was cheating. Maybe if his sister didn't help him, he wouldn't be very good, he wouldn't win all the time. Maddy blamed Simon for asking though, not her mother for telling. Asking was more the fault, she thought. It was kind of like being greedy.

O'Brien, despite Del's endorsements of his softness, proved a fiercer opponent than Simon had expected. While he suffered the hail of body blows, he retaliated by pounding away at Simon's head, opening and reopening a three-inch gash above Simon's left eye.

Whether it was Del's premonitions or Simon's youth, Kid Kahane was the winner by technical knockout. They waited for Simon outside the dressing room, Maddy suddenly tired and leaning into her father, Fram stroking her hair, his hand squatting large and heavy as a bullfrog on her head. All around them the smoke and jostle of men leaving the arena. Shirtsleeves rolled up, hats fanning broad and ruddy faces.

Maddy closes her eyes and thinks of the slim Grace O'Gorman. Her immaculate white shirt and jodhpurs. Her slickly polished boots. The red, red, red of her lips and her hair. She feels the strong arms of the aviatrix swoop her up and carry her pressed against her shoulder. The shudder of wings. The cool night air.

Simon leans back in the kitchen chair, eyes closed while Del tends the cut above his eye, carefully tracing the bloodied swelling with a cotton swab. It's after midnight and they're the only ones up in the house.

"He undid you good, that Irish boy," she says. "Wasn't as soft as I thought."

Simon winces as she pushes the skin together. He can hear the steady drip of rain through the open screen door. The far-off hush of the lake lapping against the bar. "I beat him down," he says. "Just like you told me. Tore my left up and under his ribs so many times they were mush by the fourth." Simon breathes deep, lets it out slow. "Your hands feel nice," he says. "Cool."

Del cuts a rectangle of gauze, scissors snipping through the threads of air that hold her thoughts to this kitchen. "Listen," she says. There's the distant sound of a plane. "It's those girls. Three days now."

"Willa Briggs," says Simon. "That's the one I'm teaching to box. The one who's going to teach me how to fly." He opens his eyes, watches the bandage lower to his forehead. "Maddy would like me again if I was a pilot."

It's more a question than a statement. Del pushes down gently on his head as she tapes the gauze in place. "Maddy changes her mind a lot," she says. "Now it's those girl flyers. Next year it will be something else. Don't try and keep up with her."

A plume of cool air buffets around the kitchen. Simon can smell the industrial smoke from the city chimneys. "But I do miss being Maddy's hero," he says.

Del leaves her hands on his head. She listens to the plane circling over them, a noise pitched above the chant of the rain. "Simon," she says. "Do you think they can see us? It's late. We must be the only house on the bar with a light on." She moves across to the wooden screen door and he follows her. Through the mesh of rain, only darkness. They both look up.

"There," says Del, and Simon sees, high above them, a moving star, the tiny flash of a wing light as the plane flies over the house.

J ACK DOESN'T BRING Willa and Grace any dry clothes. With their lunch on the fourth day he does send down a page of the morning's newspaper. Another invented story about the flight of the *Adventure Girl*. Grace is obviously furious, practically flings the paper across to Willa.

> RAIN DOESN'T DAMPEN GIRL FLYERS' SPIRITS
> According to Jack Robson, husband of Grace O'Gorman and pilot of the refuelling plane, the girl pilots easily weathered the storm that shook the city last night. Staying dry beneath their specially designed rain cowlings, Willa and Grace passed the time drinking hot soup and watching the spectacular show of lightning over the lake. "We're comfortable and dry," wrote Willa Briggs to Jack. "Smooth sailing."

Almost everything in the Moth is soaked from the storm. The fourth day is sunny, not too warm but hot enough to dry their wet clothes. Willa and Grace spend the day dressed only in their oilskins with their shirts, pants and underwear tied on and spread out over various parts of the rigging. The two wires on either side of the plane that angle down from the upper wing to the bottom of the fuselage under the front cockpit make excellent washing lines. They climb to five thousand feet so that no one on the ground will be able to mistake their laundry for a distress signal.

It is a hard day. With no paper or pencils there is no communication between the cockpits. This, combined with the loss of earthly detail at the increased altitude, makes the fourth day difficult to handle. Willa is amazed to find out how much she misses writing to Grace. Now, when there's no way to say anything, she finds that she has plenty to say. The only baton of language that they relay to one another during the fourth day is the signal to switch the flying rotation: one arm straight up in the air. When Grace makes this gesture at the end of her noon to 3:00 P.M. shift, Willa feels her breath go ragged in her throat.

All day the back of Grace O'Gorman, the vanishing earth. Willa's thoughts are beginning to bang into each other in her head, starting to panic for an exit. She realizes that maybe she is losing a little of her sanity, her rational mind. That maybe her emotions are being shredded by the ninety-mile-per-hour wind pushing at her all the time. There have been studies done on pilots, medical studies that determined the difference between airborne reality and earthbound reality. Willa remembers some details of an article she once read on aviation medicine. Vision is less accurate in the air than on the ground. The greater the distance between the plane and the earth, the slower the plane appears to be moving. A pilot loses all conception of a gravitational relationship with the earth, transferring this grounding allegiance to the plane itself.

Is this what is happening? thinks Willa. Has shedding the gravity of earth also altered other earthbound realities? Emotions that are used to the weighted order of the world below could be thrown into a spin at five thousand feet. A roll. A loop. Willa looks at Grace's raised arm and her heart stalls on two words.

Save me.

She wants to talk to Grace about this, find out if the emotional confusion she feels is not just confined to her. But beyond tapping Grace on the shoulder and getting her attention there is no way of making clear what she means. There is no way of explaining herself.

At this height the world becomes flat patina. The greenish bronze of the water as the sun greases it. The stains on the lake around the islands. The islands arched like a boomerang, sombre shaded and ready to be flung into the sky.

Flying is about taking the right stance in the heavens. Finding the hinge on the horizon where the sky meets the earth and slotting the plane into this groove, this track. At five thousand feet the big blank of sky curves down to meet the lake in a thin-lipped horizon. Flight is measured against a distance that is never broached. To hang in the sky a plane moves towards a horizon it can never enter, a line that just keeps receding.

It's not just gravity, thinks Willa, placing the Moth right on the etched line between water and air. It's position. It's the whole idea of where you are and what you think being somewhere is. Flight is stasis. The plane moves forward and the earth pulls back and you remain in the same place.

—————

By evening the clothes are dry and it's safe to descend again. For an hour they fly low over the harbour. Willa is anxious for detail and focuses hungrily on the squat circles of the oil tanks near the eastern gap, the braid of orange algae around the shore of the islands. She watches a coal tanker manoeuvre slowly up the shipping channel and unload by conveyor railway, adding to the black mountain range that transforms the port lands into a strange undulating elegance.

They fly over the city side and see one of the Toronto–Niagara Falls steamships leave on its evening dance cruise from the docks. Over Sunnyside they see the large wooden schooner anchored off the beach, awaiting its imminent cremation. They see the start of the baseball game, Willa's beloved Supremes going up against the Humber Bay team. The ball is a tiny white dot stitching a fast diagonal across the diamond.

As the colours of the earth leech out into blackness Willa's need to communicate with Grace fades too. They fly over the islands. At midnight there's only the moon and the halo of orange from the city. The flashing green of the light tower at the western gap. The steady red of the light tower at the eastern gap. The eight-second rotation of the lamp from the Gibraltar lighthouse on the islands. Light lying like a pale arm on the water, reaching and gone. Reaching.

And gone.

D EL TURNS THE CARDS over slowly. The young woman
across from her, hands clasped nervously in her lap,
leans forward to study the patterns of hearts and spades.

"Before we begin," says Del, flipping over the last card,
"could you give me something of yours to hold? Something
you've had for a long time."

The woman obediently removes a garnet ring, passes it
over the table to Del. "It was my mother's," she says. "Mine
since she died." She looks right at Del, the candlelight
splashing eerily against the fortune-teller's face. "She died
when I was three."

Del holds the ring inside her fist, squeezes it. The ring is
still warm from the young woman's hand.

The people that enter the fortune-teller's booth are
impressed with the cards, the crystal ball, the candles. They
expect this sort of spiritual equipment. What they don't know
is that it's all a facade. Del can see into the curve of time that
bends the past back against the future, but only when she's
holding onto something tangible, some possession that, like a
bloodhound, puts her on the trail of the person sitting opposite her. Prophecies are in the fine threads of a scarf, the worn

leather of a wallet. The future tonight is a smooth gold crescent, a dark red stone.

"You're in love," says Del. "No," she hesitates. Something brushes against the edges of her vision. "You want to be in love, but the man you've chosen doesn't want you."

The young woman expels her breath as if she's deflating, sinks back. "Why?" she asks quietly.

Del closes her eyes, concentrates on the ring in her hand. She sees a man, two men. She sees a grove of trees. The night sky.

Fortune-telling is all in the telling. There are things that people can let themselves know and things they can't. Del always tries to tell her customers the thing that is just beyond what they know to be true, so that they can let themselves stumble towards it. If there is no connection, no line between the foretold reality and the present reality, then there will be no movement towards understanding what lies ahead. It will seem too separate, too distant to belong to them and they won't believe it. The hard part for Del is not in letting customers know what is to come, but in ascertaining how much they already know, on an unconscious level, and adjusting what she has to say to meet their knowledge of the situation.

Outside the booth Del can hear the music and mechanical groans of the rides. She can hear someone hawking peanuts and beyond that the loose clackety rush of the roller coaster plummeting down its track. The screams of girls.

"What do you know of this boy?" asks Del.

The young woman leans forward again, her hands still tight together in her lap. "He's kind and charming," she says.

"He's handsome and oh so daring sometimes." She smiles at something she's remembered.

"No," says Del. "What do you *know* of him?"

There's the sound of someone running by the booth, thump of feet in the dirt.

"He works on the docks," says the girl slowly, not sure what the fortune-teller wants her to say. "He's very strong. He was born on a Monday. He likes a good night of dancing."

"He has two lives," says Del. She taps a card in front of her. "Look," she says. "It's upside down. The man you love has a secret."

"What kind of secret?" asks the young woman.

Del presses her hand tight around the ring. Why is prophecy thought of as a gift, she wonders. It isn't. What she has to say will give this woman no comfort. So often the truth is just another grief.

"He prefers the company of his own kind," she says carefully. She pauses for a moment, listens to the low call of the ferry pulling away from the docks. "In all the ways there are," she says. "It's men that he wants to be with."

———————

At midnight Del walks across the deserted amusement park, the warm night air fluid on her skin. All the crowds have evaporated. Her husband and child are asleep at home. Just the buzz of the women pilots as they drift above the islands, all that is left of the human world.

Del smokes a cigarette and walks slowly over to the Big

Spectacular Water Show. It used to be better, she thinks, passing under the painted blue arch. There used to be the tall wooden platform for the diving horse. Now there's just the big tank of strange fish, the model boats, and the indoor pool where Rose takes her clothes off underwater.

It's humid inside the pool building. Del sits up in the empty stands and watches her friend sculpt the water with her body. Rose practises her synchronized swimming after the last show, when the crowds of jeering, rowdy men have dwindled and gone. Like Del, she claims the uninhabited night, rides it there in the dark of the pool. Dolphin, Marlin, Swordfish, lazy spin of the Waterwheel. Del recognizes the patterns, loves to sit up here near the rafters and watch the watery kaleidoscope below. Catalina, Barracuda, Flamingo, Heron. The American Eiffel Tower. Rose's body as slippery as mercury. She plunges and twists, parts the water and spirals to the deep unseen bottom, all without wrinkling the surface of the pool. She is liquid, thinks Del, lighting another cigarette and watching the smoke string the wooden harp of roof above her head. She is water. No, thinks Del, she is what water wants to be.

Rose is famous for her swimming. Her shows of balletic underwater stripping entrance the crowds twice a day. All the men there for the flesh flash are surprised at the elegance, the grace of Rose's body moving in the water. The unexpected things they feel. Sometimes the men come back, bring their girlfriends and wives, say, "You've got to see this lady swim." Rose doing entire scenarios with patterns in the pool. Different costumes for different stories. The western outfit with guns, Rose coming up out of the pool, brandishing a pair of waterlogged Colts, wearing a stetson.

Rose is good at all types of water events. She always wins the women's ten-mile swim that opens the C.N.E. every year. She even holds the record for the most consecutive wins. Three. She also excels at diving, particularly high-board diving, and often competes in that. When there used to be a diving horse in the Big Spectacular Water Show she would ride him off the tower, never leaving the saddle as they both dropped eighty feet into the lake. Del remembers the excitement she always felt as the white horse ran up the tower ramp, Rose in her bathing suit, waving with one hand and holding the reins with the other. Always the fear that the horse would balk at the last minute and toss her off its back. Always she went down waving.

"Hey," says Rose. She's swum to the edge of the pool, her white bathing cap reflecting shards of moonlight that have filtered in through the windows around the top of the building. "I didn't see you up there."

Del clambers down over the folding seats to the pool edge. "Didn't want to ruin your concentration," she says.

"Who concentrates?" Rose laughs, pulls off her bathing cap, shakes her long dark hair out. "Concentration's all about staying still. Chess players concentrate." She lays her head on the wood at the side of the pool, keeps her body in the water, floating on her back. "Del," she says. "If the moon slides down right, sometimes it comes straight in those windows and washes the surface of the pool. I can swim through it and pretend I'm in the ocean."

Del sits down on the side of the pool, leaning back on her hands. She closes her eyes. She can hear the water nudging the edge of the pool, feel the thick humidity on her skin. "Have you heard from your parents yet?" she asks, opening her eyes and thinking that she was almost asleep, remembering what it was she came here to say, the wood feeling good against her hands. "My mother had a letter from the uncles. They're trying to leave." She pauses. "Fram thinks Hitler is out to get Jews."

"Fram's right," says Rose. She kicks her feet and the water froths around her. "The Germans closed my father's shop and that's the last I heard. All my letters just come back. All my questions still folded over in the envelope."

"Rose," says Del. "They're probably all right."

"You're the fortune-teller," says Rose, pushing off from the side of the pool and floating back out into the deeper water. She rolls her body, legs knifing up into the air, and disappears into the dark centre of the pool.

You tell me.

ON SATURDAY, AUGUST 5, the world below the Moth is full of activity. It's the civic-holiday weekend, a time, even in the arid economic climate, of heightened festivities. There are to be two big stage shows at Hanlan's Point on the Monday with twenty-four entertainers. Montana Frank and His Sharpshooting Outlaws are performing daily at Sunnyside. People swarm the beaches, parks and ferries.

From the plane Willa can see how everyone outside on this warm day has shut the city down. There's a blue-black welt of stopped cars along the Lakeshore, a thick stubble of humans on the pale skin of sand at Sunnyside.

It's 11:00 A.M. and already eighty degrees. Willa hopes the temperature won't push back up into the heat-wave category of late July. She has liked the cooler weather. Wearing her leather jacket at night. The crispness of the stars. She leans the plane left over the islands, thinks how easy left has become, how the plane slides that way by itself. It seems inconceivable now that she will ever bank right again. Not just the plane, she thinks. Left is the direction that her body automatically pulls as well.

Flying over the boat regatta course that defines the west side of the Hanlan's Point peninsula, Willa sees the water-beetle scuttle of the rowing shells. Rowing is the popular spectator sport in the city. Rowing and boxing. The smaller, more amateur races of this weekend are a lead-up for the big three-mile event on September 1. Single sculls. The Australian Bob Pearce pulling against the reigning champion from England, Ted Phelps. The harbour will be alive that day, she thinks, giving the Moth a little left rudder to combat the wind from the east. The whole city has been waiting all summer for that race.

Today Willa envies the people on the beaches, the people picnicking on the island parks, the simple pleasures of normal life — walking and talking. Five days in the air and her legs no longer feel as if they remember how to behave on land. Five days in the air and she has no way of communicating with her flying companion. Of the two it's talking that she misses most.

They have stopped hoping that Jack will be able to guess they need writing materials. It is obvious to Willa that he is following his own twisted counsel, intent on betraying them. Almost every day there's a fresh news article about them, things they've supposedly said and done that have nothing to do with their actual experience. When they received the first article Willa was worried that Jack would stop coming to refuel them, but now she realizes that the presence of the staffer from the *Adventure Girl* is a deterrent for that. They will continue to have fuel and food. It's everything else that is uncertain. Willa thinks that Grace must feel terrible about this, terrible and angry, but she has no way of finding out.

They're existing now as an extension of their machine. They fly the plane. They eat and excrete and sleep in short stretches. Their connection to being human is going fast. Still, there's a part of Willa that feels sympathy towards Jack Robson and his determination to hold onto the one flying achievement of his career. Who will he be without that record? An aging flying instructor working out of a temporary airport. Not very glamorous in this age of glamour aviation.

The shipping channel is clogged with coal tankers. The harbour basin sways with the small white flags of sails.

They've been flying lower than usual so they can look down. It is something to do, something to focus their attention on. Willa also spends some time taking the air temperature and timing their flying loop, though both of these activities (beyond a simple curiosity) seem pointless as there's no longer any logbook in which she can write down her findings and observations. No record of the record-breaking trip except the fabricated news articles by Jack.

Grace flies the noon to 3:00 P.M. shift and Willa attempts her daily alcohol wash, unbuttoning her shirt to swab her torso, pulling her knees up so she can get her boots off and rub her feet. The alcohol dries her skin. The air from the propeller slipstream dries her skin. The open shutter of the sun dries her skin. She spends a lot of time massaging cream into her body. It's all about trying not to make her body feel worse. Very little of her hygiene maintenance is about making her body feel better. Even her token exercising has become just a precaution against cramping muscles, not an invigorating and refreshing bout of physical activity to stimulate her body and mind. Simon Kahane would not be pleased with her loose half-hearted punches over the rear cockpit doors.

Boxing. The sound of fists thunking against a heavy bag. The stale, acrid smell of the gym. It's the only thing she remembers her father doing. Before he left, though her mother never called it that. She used to say, *Your father couldn't stay*, as if he'd been called away, was late for an appointment, would be back.

When Simon Kahane came looking for flying lessons it had seemed so right to Willa to trade learning to box with learning to fly. Just like the first time she'd seen a plane go over, straining at her mother's hand, head flapped back. She'd thought, What is that? Why am I down here?

Now the boxing, like the flying, is another bitter silence on Sunday afternoon visits at her mother's house. The only child. The big disappointment.

Just like your father.

When they've refuelled and eaten chicken legs and potato salad for lunch and it's Willa's flying shift again, Grace turns around in her seat to face her partner. They've taken to doing this over the last day and a half. Even if they can't talk or write, just to be able to see each other is a relief and a comfort.

Grace puts on fresh lipstick, fixes her hair. She's stopped wearing her flying helmet during the day — only at night for warmth — and her red hair is constantly tangling.

Willa flies and watches Grace look at herself in the small emergency mirror. She looks good, thinks Willa. I'd tell her that if I could.

It would be possible for Grace to lean right over the strip of fuselage between the cockpits and holler into Willa's ear. It would be possible for a few sentences before the effort of shouting so loudly and the awkward, dangerous position exhausted Grace. It is not worth doing. Not now when everything is running relatively smoothly. Their strength is to be guarded. Already Willa knows that pumping up from the portable fuel tins is tiring Grace. They are saving this one desperate method of communication for when there's a problem, when things are going wrong.

Grace puts away her mirror and stares at Willa. Willa stares back. The plane banks itself left over the eastern gap.

Grace spreads her arms out from her sides. All the way out.

What is she doing? thinks Willa.

The Moth pulls left over the city.

Grace tilts her arms slightly in imitation of the bank.

Plane.

Willa nods to show she understands.

Grace turns her wrists so that her hands move from palm down to sideways with the thumb edge facing up. Her arms are still out at her sides.

Climb.

She twists her wrists so that her thumbs point down.

Dive.

She banks her arms left, then right.

Bank.

Willa nods and nods. The words pop and crackle in the space between the cockpits.

Grace points to herself, taps her breastbone with her right forefinger.

I.

She points to her lips, oiled red from the lipstick.

Kiss? thinks Willa. She shakes her head in confusion.

Grace opens her mouth and closes it, mimics speech.

Willa nods.

Grace reaches across and touches Willa gently on the side of the face.

Cheek. Lips. Breast.

Body. Mouth. Body.

I will talk to you.

They lose track of time. Willa flies right through Grace's early-evening rotation and they don't notice. She flies almost without looking at the earth at all. Hanging on her line in the sky by feel, by the fingerholds of repetition. She only has Grace in her sights. Grace, sitting backwards, cross-legged in her seat, forming them a language out of air.

When they move beyond the parts and functions of the plane it becomes more difficult to convey meanings. They spend a long time over each word, learning and relearning it to the point of nausea and then they move on to a new one. Grace often has to think for a while between each invented signal, trying to figure out what to say and the best way of saying it. Slowly they build an elemental vocabulary.

Earth: Left arm out, palm up.

Water: Undulating the right hand up and down like the movement of a snake.

Sky: Sign for *earth* but with the right hand making an invisible arc above the outstretched palm of the left hand.

Wind: Moving the fingers of the right hand when the hand is out in front of the body, palm down. The fingers trilling the air in imitation of the motion of wind.

Rain: Holding both hands up above the head, fingers pointing down towards the hair and wiggling to show the drops of rain.

Pieces of clothing and parts of the body are signed by pointing to them. Grace signals food by first pointing to her open mouth and then trying to imitate by pantomime a particular kind of food. Thumb and forefinger closed together in the oval of an egg. An imaginary chicken leg grasped in a fist and gnawed on. Coffee indicated by coughing followed by the motion of drinking slowly from a mug.

Until they bump up against the blunt edge of darkness and Grace's hands begin to blur, they keep describing and identifying, hoarding the names of things.

It is not like ordinary talking, thinks Willa, when Grace has finally turned around in her cockpit and has taken over the controls of the Moth.

It is learning to talk in a different way.

Maddy bicycles under the Moth. It's flying low today and she can see the white of the pilots' shirts, their hair gnarled with wind. She rides along the boardwalk on the northern shore of the islands, the wood mumbling under her wheels. All the way to the edge of the eastern channel and then all the way back again to the base of Hanlan's. Once when she's pedalling east and once when she's pedalling west the plane passes above her. She puts her head back to watch it, spreads her arms out from the bicycle, palms down.

It's early Sunday morning and the boardwalk is deserted. Most of the islands' residents are either still in bed or getting ready for church. Her father, she thinks, just this moment is probably changing into his one good suit, polishing his old black shoes. Maddy is glad that she doesn't have to go to church. That is the one good thing about being her mother's daughter, being Jewish. She has been spared any religious training. Del observes some of the Jewish rituals and holidays, mainly for her parents' sake, but she is by no means guided by any kind of faith or doctrine. Even so she refuses to let Fram take her daughter into the Presbyterian church and raise her as a Christian. This is completely suitable to Maddy, who has no interest in any god except for the almighty Grace O'Gorman.

Maddy reaches the eastern channel and rests for a moment, straddling the bar on her black bicycle, feet down flat on the wooden boardwalk. Across the narrow belt of water there are the light towers, steady red. Beyond that the bumpy black hills of coal. She checks the position of the Moth. It's just banking past the city, a bruise in the pale morning sky.

Sometimes, early, when everything on the islands is quiet, Maddy can hear the dim, distant noises of the city, like something heard underwater. The muffled clang of a church bell. The far-away slide of a train whistle. Now, as she stares out over the eastern gap at the port lands, she hears only the faint buzzing of the plane.

Maddy cycles back towards Hanlan's, the lake on her left side, the main bulk of the islands on her right. The wood says a slow prayer beneath her rubber tires. Just as she's passing Sunfish Island she sees the Moth flying towards her, a dark double line above the trees. The plane comes nearer and she sees something small arch up out of the cockpit and come spinning through the air, landing on the boardwalk about a hundred feet in front of her. Maddy races forward. The Moth skips over her head and drones its way to the east.

Apple core. Shiny white on the brown planks. Mostly eaten but still some flesh around the ends. Maddy squats down beside it. The stem's still attached. One of the seeds pokes its brown snout out of the core. There's a small pink stain near the bottom. Lipstick. Maddy picks up the apple carefully, turns it over in her hand. She lifts it to her mouth, kisses it and then drops it into the right front pocket of her trousers.

———

Maddy lies on her stomach in the grass behind a clump of bushes on Sunfish Island. A few hundred feet in front of her hiding place are the canvas bunkhouses of the working boys' camp. There's no one outside the buildings, no sound from within. Charred logs lie in the big firepit in the centre of the horseshoe of tents.

Probably all asleep, thinks Maddy. She's pretty sure that the working boys aren't made to go to church. Too early for the little cowards, she thinks grimly, pulling a folded piece of paper from her back trouser pocket. She spreads it flat on the still dew-damp grass and reads it for the fourth time since Miro cut it out of yesterday's paper and gave it to Fram to take home to her.

FIVE DAYS AND COUNTING
The girl pilots have circled in the sky over our fair
city for five full days now and show no signs of
tiring. They have made an estimated 720 loops over
the harbour, with approximately 2,880 still to go
before they land at the C.N.E. on August 25. "We're
so used to the sound of their plane," says one local
resident, "that we don't bother to look up any more
when they fly over."

There's the sound of someone walking around at the camp. Maddy looks up quickly to see a boy in pyjamas come just in front of where she is lying and sit down on an upended log. He's cradling something in his hands. He settles in profile to Maddy and bends over the object he holds, adjusting something, moving something. It's a plane. A model plane. A tiny, wooden Moth. Maddy holds her breath and watches as the boy notches the upper wings forward so they're staggered over the lower set.

"Too much," she blurts out before she can stop herself.

The boy startles, half rises off the log, but sits back down again when he sees who's talking. "What are you doing?" he says, staring at her.

"What are *you* doing?" says Maddy with more authority. She scrambles up and goes over to him, taps his wooden plane. "You've made the upper wings too far forward. In a real Moth," she says bossily, "the upper wings are only three and a half inches ahead of the lower ones."

The boy looks quizzically at her. "How do you know that?" he asks.

Maddy puffs out her chest. "I know everything about Moths," she says. "I am knowledgeable on the subject." She looks hard at this brown-haired boy in his red pyjamas. She thinks he might be one of the boys who was trespassing on her barge-plane the other day. One of those nosy, prying, bumping, climbing, pushing boys who were trying to get inside her secret place. "If you don't know how to do it," she says, "then you shouldn't be doing it."

"I'm entering a contest," says the boy. "So I have to get it right."

"What contest?"

"The C.N.E. model airplane contest," says the boy. "I have to have my plane in before the twentieth. I've been working on it in the mornings before the others get up."

Maddy has heard nothing about any model plane contest at the C.N.E. Maybe there's still time for her to build a perfect Moth with the upper wings three and a half inches in front of the lower ones.

"How do I enter?" she asks eagerly.

"Enter?" The boy looks at her as if she's just said something incomprehensible. "Oh," he says finally, "it's just for boys."

"Boys?" Maddy can't believe it. "Are you sure?"

"Of course I'm sure." The boy stands up. He's taller than she is by at least a foot. Taller and bigger. She backs up a little. "The contest is just for boys and this camp is just for boys." He starts to move off, turns around when he's by the firepit. "But," he says, "I'll check what you said about the wings."

Maddy watches him go back inside his tent. She scuffs her feet through the grass, her shoes all wet by the time she gets back to her bicycle. She rides slowly away from Sunfish Island, back along the boardwalk towards Hanlan's. The wood sputters like a bad engine beneath her wheels.

The shadow of the plane passes over her. She doesn't look up.

WILLA AND GRACE spend most of the next day working on their invented language. Flying has become something that happens in the background; like breathing, it's automatic and barely noticed. The plane seems to know what to do without them paying attention to it.

Grace sits facing Willa as they ride the blue sky, the sun on their left side, right side, warming their backs.

It has been fairly easy to invent and communicate single descriptive words that they already inhabit, movements of the plane, the naming of earth, water and wind. But for them to move beyond simply identifying things into some kind of dialogue, some kind of conversation, they need to know not just the names of things, but intellectual concepts. This proves harder than Willa imagined. Sitting in her cockpit watching the frenetic hand-waving of Grace, she feels that it's all a rather desperate party game. Two words — four syllables — sounds like . . .

They finally get an interrogative sign. Both hands outstretched, palms up, shoulders shrugged and a questioning look on the face.

What?

This one question can also be used to stand in for all the other question words — *what* as *why, when, which, who, how* and *where. What place? What you? What to do this?*

This second day they have the process for signing down pat. Grace first signals the upcoming sign by connecting it with a sign that they've already learned. A word associated with earth, with water, with sky. A word tied to a part or function of the body. She then tries to invent a sign that carries some of the meaning of the word in pantomime. The fingers drizzling down on the top of the head for the falling rain. The up and down of waves. Then, having done all she can to translate what it is she is saying, she waits for Willa to guess correctly. The more complex the words become, the harder Willa finds this is to do. For Willa to recognize a concept like time from Grace's sweeps and curves, she has to see it as Grace would see it, imagine how she thinks. The more complicated the signing, the more of a stretch Willa must make, the more she must rely on what she knows of this woman in the front of the plane. She is learning a way to talk but she is also learning how Grace thinks. She is finding out that the flamboyance she always associated with Grace O'Gorman is not there. Grace is methodical with the signing, detailed, seemingly aware of both what she wants to say and what she thinks will be understood. She appears to be thinking of Willa, and Willa, unused to anyone's positive attention, feels almost dizzy from this kindness.

Willa has often indicated *time* by tapping the face of her watch, but now they have a movement for it, a shape carved out of air. Grace first showing the sign for *day* — her closed right fist arcing from east to west to demonstrate the sun moving across the sky — and then circling her fist around her upright left index finger. The sun circling a static object, a tree perhaps. Grace makes this sign and Willa thinks how perfectly right it is. Time as moving and as still. The stiff elegance of the static. The unseen shadow draping itself over the tree and staining the ground. The circling motion also reminiscent of string being wound around a finger. For the first time Willa sees what they are making not just as a substitute for words, but something instead of, better than words. She likes that language is now something that happens with hands and eyes and not with ears. She likes it that words take up space in the air. A physical presence. The body as the word.

Once Willa and Grace have a word for *time* they are able to express more concepts. Grace, aware that she has Willa's complete focus and that Willa is responding to the signing, works in earnest. She has found something, by accident, that will make the flight bearable, will make the flight possible. If she can keep Willa interested in this language, then Willa won't surrender to her obvious fatigue. Grace shapes her mind around the word *time*. The past or history is *back time*, Grace indicating *time* and then gesturing behind her body. The future is *ahead time*, Grace pointing forward. Memory or remembering is *head time*, Grace tapping her temple after signing *time*. There's *daytime* and *not daytime* (Grace shaking her head *no* before signing *day*) for night. There's *not daytime sun* for moon. There's *morning* and *afternoon*, Grace's sun fist at different positions in the sky to indicate the appropriate time.

The concept of time opens up more windows for them than any other word so far.

It is not until this second day of signing, when patterns have become established, that Willa realizes the roles that have been assigned and accepted in this new language they're creating. Grace signs and Willa responds. Because of the positioning in the plane, the two cockpits with Willa always behind Grace, Grace talks to Willa while Willa flies the plane. When Grace is flying the plane there's no communication. It also means that Willa can make minimal replies as she has to keep control of the stick. The more complex their language becomes, the more it effectively excludes Willa from participating. Grace will soon be able to sign phrases while Willa will only be able to squeeze out the odd word. She'll only be able to do one-handed words. As the day spins on, Willa becomes increasingly aware that their signing is really about Grace talking to Willa.

The *not daytime sun* rises at 7:56 in the evening. Full like the night before, bulging like a milky eye in the dark sky. With such a moon it's almost as bright as daylight. The world below the plane shimmers in iridescent fish scales.

Willa is grateful for the moon. It makes the ten o'clock refuelling a much easier feat. The days when it's cloudy, even though the monoplane shines a big light down from the cabin, it's difficult to see the hose, to fumble it into the tank. It's difficult to keep the Moth clipped onto the same rotation as Jack's plane.

Tonight the moon wipes a film over the two planes, the length of rubber hose, the white swaying canvas bundle. Tonight Grace swoops up the cargo on the first attempt, undoes the bag. The moon slivers off the shiny metal of the fuel tins, lines of light skidding on the fuselage.

In their supply bag there are some clean shirts and underwear along with the supper of baked beans, buns, apples, dried dates and the thermos of coffee. Good for the *Adventure Girl* staffer, thinks Willa. She can't imagine that it's Jack who's worried about their underwear.

Willa feels exhausted, a tiredness that coats the usual numbing fatigue with a heavy stickiness. It's hard to lift her arms, hard to keep her head upright. She eats and feels a little better. Snuggles into the soft warmth of her jacket. Sips coffee and watches the stars. Everything bright tonight. The stars like beads strung across the night sky. So tired and she can't even sleep.

In the beginning of the flight Willa could distinguish between waking and sleeping. Waking was the uncomfortable, reasonably alert portion of the day. Sleeping was the solidly unconscious, no dreams, not knowing it had happened until awake. There were distinctions. They felt different. Now Willa is aware she exists in a state that's somehow between waking and sleeping and she's lost a lot of the early discomfort of the flight, but she's also lost the ability to differentiate properly between physical states. Everything has levelled out into a bearable flatness and, for her to notice or feel anything, conditions have to develop to extremes. She doesn't notice discomfort, but she can still feel pain. She knows that what she's experiencing is a result of being in the air for six days. She has heard lots of stories about long-distance voyages on land or sea where people went mad from the various stresses on the body. The danger of going to extremes was that sometimes you couldn't find your way back.

Willa thinks of her little cabin at the Air Harbour, tries to imagine the furniture, the books on the shelves. She tries to remember her life on the ground, but it seems so far away. Up here she's closer to the heavens than she is to earth. She finishes her coffee, screws the cap back onto the body of the thermos. She leans forward, pulls down the collar of Grace's leather jacket so that the back of her neck is exposed. With her right index finger she slowly spells words on Grace's skin.

Don't let me go crazy.

The moon is pale and vast. The stars so sharp they almost hurt.

ON THE CIVIC-HOLIDAY Monday something goes wrong with the plane. At a point where Willa hears the engine as if it vibrates through her blood and takes for granted that the Moth is solid earth, the fragile mechanics of the plane become all too apparent.

It's a small thing. A pin. The clevis pin comes loose from the base of the stick and Willa suddenly has no control of the plane. The stick goes slack and she looks down and sees the small steel pin roll backwards under her seat. For a moment the Moth continues its level flight, but at the time they need to turn over the city it just keeps flying straight. Willa leans forward and yells into Grace's ear.

"I can't fly."

Her voice feels strange and she thinks that it must sound all creaky, like a rusty hinge.

"Clevis pin's come loose."

Grace nods and banks the Moth sharply left, heading back towards the water.

Willa scrabbles under her seat but she can't feel the tiny piece of metal. She hopes it hasn't rolled right back into the tail. Such a little thing and it affects so much. Of course they don't have an extra one. They don't carry many extra anythings. That's what Jack is for — to answer all their needs. Such a perfect system, thinks Willa sarcastically, trying not to panic and twisting her body in the cockpit so that her head is down on the floor and her legs dangle over the port door. She gropes around with her hands but can't feel anything, bangs her head on the stick.

"Shit," she says, still upside down and imagining she's been eaten by some movie monster, her legs kicking up a dramatic ballet into the air.

She swivels herself back into the upright world, feeling a little dizzy, and leans into Grace again.

"It's under the seat."

Already her throat is sore from yelling.

"It needs to roll out."

Grace nods and pulls back hard on her stick, lifting the nose of the Moth into a steep climb. They pass two thousand, then three thousand, hit four thousand feet. Grace sends the plane into a dive and Willa, unprepared for the steepness of the angle, lurches forward into the small windscreen and bangs her head again.

It's almost noon and the plane is relatively empty of fuel. With the weight low, Grace is able to go into her trademark range of acrobatic manoeuvres. She dives straight down towards the water, pulls up and starts rocking the plane from side to side. The clevis pin is now visible and rolling back and forth, up and down the curved sides of the cockpit fuselage. Willa manages to grab it finally when it's near her right foot and brandishes it in front of Grace's face to show that she can stop the stunting.

But Grace doesn't stop. She zooms up into the heavens again, puts the plane into a stall and slides sideways across the grey sky. Willa clips herself hurriedly into her safety harness in case Grace forgets that they're not strapped in and heads into some spins or loops. It would be embarrassing to fall out of the plane.

Willa holds the clevis pin tightly in her fist, waiting for Grace to fly normally again and allow her to put it back in place. She's never been much of a stunter and it unnerves her a little to be in a plane that's bucking and kicking on its axis. She's annoyed with Grace for this display of acrobatics. Willa likes a more sedate pace to flying. It's being in the air that she likes, not chewing it up with wings. Her dream is to be able to get a job that will keep her in the air all day, every day. Nice steady flying work, ferrying people or sacks of mail from place to place. Different scenes to look down on, different weather to accommodate. None of this wrapping the plane around pillars of air. But she knows that this is Grace's idea of flying — stunting or record-setting. Before Grace became so famous she was renowned as a barnstormer, putting down in farmers' fields and performing for change for a small crowd of local people. The stories say that she always flew with an evening gown as her only luggage, so that if she was invited out for dinner she could go in style.

Grace drops the plane level again and after Willa has bent down and twisted the clevis pin back into the base of her stick she takes control and pulls the Moth back into its slow sweep of city, water, islands. Grace turns in her seat and her face is flushed. She touches her lips, her chest over her heart, and opens the fingers of a closed fist into the air as though they're releasing something up towards the sun.

I feel good.

Seeing Grace's happiness, Willa can no longer be angry with her.

It is a dull day for a holiday. Cloudy with tantrums of rain every now and then, small feet stamping down from the sky. It's humid and muggy, moisture everywhere. Willa spends most of the day damp from rain or sweat.

The civic-holiday weekend is the big holiday of the summer. People are intent on celebration. Willa and Grace watch the overloaded ferries glide to and fro across the bay, bringing thousands of people to the islands for the extravagant stage shows and the usual rides and attractions.

Willa is glad that the islands are getting lots of the holiday trade. She has always preferred them to Sunnyside (except for the women's baseball games on the diamond near the Sunnyside Bathing Pavilion). She used to go to the Hanlan's Point Amusement Park with her father when she was young. They'd sit on the upper deck of the old Maple Leaf Stadium and watch the men row their shells along the length of the regatta course, oars stringing the water behind the boats in thin beaded lines.

They fly over Sunnyside, and Willa sees people on the decks of the *Lyman M. Davis*. She knows from the newspapers that Jack's sent down that there have been protests about burning this last of the Great Lakes schooners and that it has been granted a temporary reprieve while they let the public board it. No promises that it still won't be put to spark, but for now the holiday thirst for fire is being transferred to an old wooden steamer off Centre Island.

Later at night, when the sun has gone down and the moon is dim light behind the clouds, they see the thrash of flame from below. Willa takes them low and they can feel the updraft from the burning boat, scorched breath heating the underside of the fuselage so that the fire is something they feel beneath their feet. It's so hot in the plane that they just wear their thin white shirts and jodhpurs. No jackets. They tighten their circle and fly around and around the bonfire. Willa is careful to rise a little as the updraft affects the handling of the Moth. They can't see people but they can see the slippery orange of trees along the shore illuminated by the burning steamer. They can see sparks as parts of the boat collapse, wood falling onto wood, the shift sending patterns of flame into the air.

Grimy sweat runs down Willa's face. She wipes her forehead with her arm, traces letters onto Grace's back.

People love watching fire and water.

The bonfire, the boats to Niagara Falls twice a day. The intricate lace of summer storms over a lake. It's as though, thinks Willa, we can't imagine anything beyond the power of fire or water. They answer something in us, something we've forgotten how to ask.

The flames seem huge, seem to lap up and sear the inside of Willa's throat. Her tongue sticks to the top of her mouth. Her nostrils feel charred inside.

You fly like that burns, she writes on Grace and Grace reaches back after the final *s* and holds onto Willa's hand. They fly through the flames again, the Moth buzzing over the glow, wings dipping in supplication above the fiery earth.

M ADDY IS HELPING Miro dress, squeezing his flesh into the strict confines of the blue-and-white sailor suit. Pants. Shirt with brass buttons and a wide collar. Jaunty cap with a nautical blue bow festooning the front. It's hard work and they're both sweating from the exertion. In the corner of the living room the radio crackles out "Boulevard of Broken Dreams."

"Too bloody hot to be naval," grumbles Miro as Maddy tries to yank the blue cotton pants up to his waist.

"You got fatter," she says accusingly.

Miro, standing in the middle of his tiny living room, starts to sway with the force of Maddy's efforts. "I'm supposed to be fat," he says. "It's my job."

"Fat," says Maddy between clenched teeth, "but not fatter." She struggles for a few more moments and then collapses on the floor, lying flat on her back, arms up above her head.

Miro has the sailor shirt on, his puffy chest straining against the anchor buttons. The pants, however, are only up as far as mid-thigh. His white underwear looks like a giant bandage on the middle of his body. He waddles a little forward, but can't move properly because of the constriction of the trousers.

"Maddy," he says, "I'm getting tired of standing. You can't leave me like this."

Maddy eyes him from her position on the floor. "You got fatter," she says. "That's not my problem." She looks up at the cobwebbed ceiling of the little bungalow. "And," she says. "I'm doing this out of my kind heart."

Miro snorts. "You talk like a relief worker," he says. "Kind heart, my ass."

Maddy jerks up onto her knees, leans over and bites his bum hard through the white cotton underwear.

Miro yelps and almost falls. Maddy jumps up and blocks his descent with her body, holding him upright and steady. They are locked together.

"You torture me," says Miro into Maddy's shoulder.

"I like to," she says gently, before she pushes him away from her embrace.

Miro lies on pillows in his sailor suit in a giant pram with a fringed canopy and wooden signs on both sides that say "King of All Fat Babies." There's a small box for coins attached to the front of the baby carriage. Fram pushes Miro, and Maddy walks beside her father as they wheel the corpulent dwarf across the grounds of the amusement park.

It's the evening of the holiday Monday and there are crowds of people about. More people than they've seen at

Hanlan's for a long time. Everywhere there's the noise of voices and the swoosh of rides, the crack, crack of rifles shooting for glass vases or dolls with eyes that open and close.

Fram has left the carousel in the care of Jim, his helper, and is taking his family and Miro to see the big stage show in the pavilion.

He pushes the pram up to Del's fortune-telling hut.

"Go see if your mother's coming," he says to Maddy and she runs around to the front of the hut, listening by the curtain to see if she can hear voices. Nothing. She pushes through the heaviness and enters the dark interior. Her mother, smoking a cigarette, immediately moves to hide it and then, seeing who it is in the doorway, laughs in relief.

"Only you," she says.

Maddy walks over to the table with the crystal ball and the playing cards. The candle flame flickers from the air her body displaces. "Dad wants to know if you're coming to the big show at the pavilion."

"Oh," says Del. "I'm not taken with the piper like your father. I don't think I'm ready for the call of the Highlands just yet. I'll work for a while — it's a good night so far — and then I'll join you later at the bonfire. Is that agreeable?"

She reaches over the table and touches her daughter on the arm. Maddy allows this gesture only for a moment before pulling away.

"Do you hate Scottish people?" she asks.

Del drops her cigarette on the dirt floor, grinds it out with her foot. "No," she says slowly. "Of course not. I married Fram now, didn't I?"

"I don't think people from different places should marry," says Maddy.

"You can't think that," returns Del sharply. "You wouldn't exist if Fram and I had thought like that."

"I'm not Jewish," says Maddy, her hand trickling over the smooth surface of the crystal ball. "I'm Canadian."

"Go tell your father I'll meet you later," says Del.

"Can you see the pilots?" asks Maddy, her hand still hovering on the crystal ball.

"No," says Del, her voice soft and even. "You know how I work. I need to touch things before I can see anything. Now go on, Maddy."

They look at each other across the cluttered table in the small dark hut. Del smiles a small, rueful smile.

"You may not be Jewish," she says, "but it's me that you're like."

Fram, in a great excitement about the Scottish bagpiper, uses Miro's carriage as a battering ram to gain a good position by the stage. Miro shakes his rattle vigorously to signal people out of their way.

By the time the piper takes the stage Maddy is thoroughly sick of the show. She's seen singers and jugglers and a special dog that could do a lot of human feats. She can't even pretend to be enthusiastic when the piper begins his mournful blasts. Miro too is bored, leans over the side of his carriage and whispers to Maddy, "Sounds like a constipated cow."

Fram, however, is ecstatic. "Lovely," he says at the first long howl of the pipes. He rests against the handle of the carriage, mumbling endearments, tears coursing down his cheeks.

It is a little embarrassing. Maddy is glad that it's fairly dark inside the pavilion and other people can't see what a sentimental idiot her father is.

"*Six* constipated cows," she says conspiratorially to Miro. "And one elephant with diarrhea."

———————

Maddy stands beside her mother on the edge of Mugg's Island, watching the old wooden steamer on fire. It burns fast, the air spitting with sparks, the flames climbing invisible ladders into the night sky.

Fram has taken Miro home and will be back in time to see only a shadow of ashes on the moon-shiny lake.

The shore of the island is clogged with people. Maddy keeps getting pushed forward, knocked by elbows. The crowd is rowdy, yells and whistles as the old boat sputters away. A group of men are passing a bottle around. Some people are breaking branches off nearby trees and hurling them out into the flames. Trees sway and shudder as they are pushed and pulled, branches crack, leaves rattle above Maddy's head. She watches a screaming man dragged to the water's edge by three other men and tossed in. One of the pursuers jumps in after his victim and they wrestle each other in the muddy shallows.

"I don't like the way this city delights in burning things," says Del.

Maddy doesn't reply, but she doesn't disagree. She feels sorry for the old boat and she worries about her barge in Blockhouse Bay. Couldn't some of these boats be fixed? They're old, but some of them, like this one, still float. Wouldn't they still work?

Above the yells of the crowd and the pops of the fire Maddy hears the thin rasp of the plane. She looks up and sees the Moth flitting through the dark sky, circling the flames.

SIMON WALKS purposefully across the concrete floor of the hangar towards the sound of metal on metal coming from the back of the building. He knows his way around the airport, all those weeks coming for Willa's boxing lessons. He jabs at the air in front of him, just once, as he passes the spot where the heavy bag rests on its chain.

"You Jack Robson?" he asks the man bent over a damaged biplane, tapping something with a wrench.

The man looks round, lays his wrench carefully down on the lower wing, wipes his hands on his pants. "Yeah?" he says.

"This is for you." Simon passes over a white envelope. "Well, it's not really for you. It's for Air Ace Grace. Your wife."

"My wife," repeats Jack dully.

"A letter," says Simon. "From my niece, Maddy. She's a big fan of this endurance flight, of your wife. We were hoping that you'd be able to take it up to her when you next go to refuel them."

Simon is surprised at how old Jack Robson seems to be. He'd expected that Air Ace Grace would have been married to some young, dashing gentleman of the air, not this run-down flight instructor.

"I'm Simon Kahane," he says. "I was teaching Willa Briggs to box. Right over there." He points back towards the large, heavy bag.

"The boxer," says Jack, not looking where Simon is pointing. "Yeah, I've seen you fight. Bet money on you."

"Did you win?"

Jack hears the tiny tin buzz of the Moth up in the sky above the hangar. "Can't remember," he says.

"Oh." Simon is disappointed. He stands there a moment longer, waiting for Jack to say something else. "Oh well," he says finally. "I promised Maddy I'd bring you that letter. She spent all last night writing it." He turns and begins walking slowly back across the hangar, turns when he's a little way from the plane. "How many days have they been up now?"

"Eight," mutters Jack, standing motionless by the plane.

"That's something, isn't it," says Simon. He grins, jabs the air in front of him a couple of times and walks back towards the door, back outside into the morning sun.

Jack looks down at the envelope in his hand. "Please Deliver to Grace O'Gorman" printed in an awkward child script across the front. He slowly crumples it up, walks purposefully over to a metal trash container and tosses it in.

Jack sits in the cabin of the monoplane. He's untied the plane from its hold on the tarmac, checked the aileron and rudder controls. It's the moment just before he will start the engine and manoeuvre the plane down the runway and into the sky.

It is the last moment to hear the sounds of the world before the engine kicks everything else out of the way. Outside the plane there's the chatter of birds and the occasional drawl of a gull. Inside the plane there's the noise of Fred in the cargo space behind Jack's seat, securing the ropes onto the canvas bag of supplies for *Adventure Girl*.

Jack wishes he could remain in this moment before flight. This moment when the idea of flight, the anticipation of being in the air, is combined with the casual rhythms of the earth. He could have it all.

He taxis the monoplane down the runway, jerks it up into a blue sky and aims upwards towards the Moth. He thinks that they're getting tired. In the past couple of days they've had really erratic altitudes — sometimes brushing the ceiling of the sky, sometimes a mere five hundred feet above the ground. He knows that a need for extremes or a sense of extremes as the norm is a sign of fatigue.

Jack pulls his plane into the space above the Moth and circles with them over the islands. Looking down he can see Willa in the rear cockpit and Grace struggling into her catching-the-bag position, almost standing and bracing herself back against the wings. He can't tell anything about her from up here. She wears her usual white long-sleeved shirt. She has no helmet on, but brown leather gloves on her hands. He can't see her face, the lines on her forehead, the shadows of exhaustion pooling beneath her eyes. She doesn't look up. From here she could be anyone. Not his wife, most definitely not his wife.

"It's going," yells Fred from behind him, and the cabin door opens and the bag plummets down to Grace. She struggles it into her plane. Jack watches her untie it, pull the hose into the hollow of the wing tank. Fred releases the fuel from the big cabin tank, opens the valve to let it flow down the black rubber hose.

Jack is connected to his wife only through this long, dangling rubber hose.

When the refuelling is finished and Fred is winding in the length of hose, the anchor of canvas bag full of empty fuel tins, Jack watches Grace unpack the lunch of cold chicken and potato salad. He watches her pull a newspaper from the bundle of clean clothes and food. What do they think of what he's done? He knows that Grace hates being misquoted, is always trying to stay the press's darling so they'll treat her kindly. It must make her furious to be handed down these invented stories. But she still doesn't look up. She doesn't look for him out of anger, gratitude, love. He is just part of this necessary process of refuelling her plane, part of what enables her another eight hours of flying in a circle, another eight hours closer to breaking his record.

Jack hasn't given himself one solid reason as to why he's writing the articles about Grace and Willa. He hasn't named anything for himself, even though he's felt it all — jealousy, envy, frustration, rage, loneliness. The one thing he has acknowledged is his desire for a reaction from Grace. He wants her to look up, shake a fist. Do something to show that he's made some sort of impact on her. That she's noticed him. But there is no response from the *Adventure Girl*.

Fred pulls in the canvas bag and closes the cargo door. The noise of air whirlpooling around the opening suddenly stops and everything seems deathly quiet.

"All in," says Fred. There's the sound of him coiling up the fuel hose to lay on top of the big metal gas tank. The canvas bag he'll leave for Jack to open — in case there are any private messages from his wife. Fred would be surprised, Jack thinks, to know there are never any messages, that Grace can't be bothered to write to him.

Jack takes a last look down before pulling his plane out of the Moth's gravity. Wings. The shape of Willa in the rear cockpit. The name *Adventure Girl* bannered across the side of the fuselage. Barely visible amid a tangle of rigging wires and struts, his wife, doing such an ordinary thing, eating a leg of cold, fried chicken, and wrecking his life.

———

Jack sits at a table in the lunchroom at the airport, trying to write the Grace and Willa quotes for tomorrow's article. Even though he's seen all of Grace's press clippings and knows the style of the writing, it gets harder and harder to think of what to say. What they're experiencing becomes more and more distant to him. He tries to think of what his own endurance flight was like but he can no longer remember the specifics. What he knows of it now are the broad arcs — fatigue, boredom, routine. All the details have been swept up into these clumsy piles.

Grace.

He's not sure he can even remember her properly. He does know the details — she likes toast for breakfast, she likes a nap in the afternoons. But what he's missing is a way to put them together into a larger picture. Who is Grace O'Gorman? Jack is not sure that he knows, or ever knew. She doesn't talk about herself much. Only what she intends to do, only action. Nothing that she thinks.

Jack puts his head down on his arms. He misses sleeping next to her. The smell of her skin in the morning. The sound of her breathing. He misses the light way she talked to him, never letting him get too down on himself. She was his champion because he couldn't do it himself, he thinks, his head down near the cold metal of the table. Now that she's gone he just can't keep up with her idea of him. He's fallen back into someone he doesn't even recognize. Someone who invents his wife every day. Someone who believes that she's not coming back to earth. Not coming back to save him.

PAIN IN THE PLANE

The twenty-five-day endurance flight of Grace O'Gorman and Willa Briggs over the city of Toronto was almost called off yesterday night when Grace developed acute appendicitis and could no longer pilot the plane. She lay slumped over the side of her cockpit while the more inexperienced Willa Briggs attempted to tend to her partner and fly the Moth DH60T in constant circles over the harbour.

"It was tough-going there for a while," said an exhausted Willa in a note to Jack Robson in the refuelling plane. "But we hung on."

It is thought that Grace O'Gorman spent much of the night unconscious, but seems almost fully recovered this morning.

"We're staying up," she says.

Such a determined pair of girls.

Willa quite enjoys reading the morning's article, has to remind herself, *Oh yes, that's us.* She likes the drama of the appendicitis attack, imagines Grace lying back in an elegant faint, head lolling on the fuselage while she, Willa, wipes the patient's fevered brow with a wet cloth. Jack's story is not without its attractions. Grace, though, makes a cross over her heart after reading the article to show that she hates what he's doing, hates the idea of herself in a weakened condition. And Willa knows how much Grace would loathe depending on someone to take care of her. She understands why Jack wrote her in as the sick one — he knows that about Grace too.

Willa drinks her morning coffee while Grace flies the plane. She watches the sun notch up on the horizon, pooling over the blue square of water. She likes the sunrise, is never bored by its beauty. Morning is her favourite part of the day, the only time that she feels alert and awake.

Willa peels an orange, tosses the corkscrew of casing over the side of the Moth. Nine days. She takes stock of her body, as she does every morning. Skin — a bit dry and sunburned on her face and hands, but relatively painless. Legs — stiff and sometimes numb. Even with her exercise routine of pulling her knees up to her chest and back down under the fuselage again, the muscles seem atrophied and weak. Feet — also sometimes numb from working the rudder pedals and at night they're often cold, even in double socks. Rear end — sore from sitting so long. Neck — all right this morning, but often so stiff that she spends part of each day with a headache. There is no comfortable position to sleep in and her head is often twisted over the back of her cockpit, vibrating against the metal of the fuselage. Eyes — dry from the constant torrent of the slipstream and tired from looking into the sun. Both Willa and Grace have stopped wearing their goggles all the time because the pressure against their eye sockets grew too painful. Willa will sometimes wear her tinted pair of goggles though, just to keep the sun out of her eyes. Back — stiff but not too bad. Arms and hands — fine and functional. Her appetite is good and she enjoys all the meals, even though her clothes seem baggier and she suspects that she's losing weight. She could use a bath or a better way of cleaning herself. The alcohol they use to wash themselves dries her skin. She could use a walk and a full-course meal and a good night's sleep, but she doesn't long for any of these things uncontrollably. If she never had any of them again, it would be a loss but she wouldn't grieve. To live in the sky seems far greater than a clean change of clothes.

Willa sometimes wonders if anyone on earth thinks of her. Perhaps her mother, to worry about Willa crashing and dying, thinking of the funeral expenses. Perhaps the other instructors at the airfield, curious as to how she's faring up here in the ether for so long. Now that she's above her life it appears very small to Willa, diminished. She spends most of her time at the airfield, tolerated by the men but excluded from their easy camaraderie. She sees her mother once a week, taking a streetcar out to the east end of the city for a largely unpleasant afternoon. School friends have fallen away. Willa realizes that perhaps, on that earth below, there is no one who really loves her.

Willa and Grace never ask how the other is doing. They take it for granted that they are experiencing the same things, the same feelings and responses to their environment. What they talk about in Grace's fluid sign language and Willa's finger-writing is not how they are, but who they are. Grace indicating to Willa how much her first flight had meant to her, the feeling of that so much closer now that they are in the sky. Willa, last night, spelling out on Grace's skin the first time she went up in a plane by herself and got lost. Landing in a field to ask the farmer where she was. No compass, figuring she would just recognize the earth from above.

The first stories that Willa and Grace tell each other are flying stories. The first things they want to say about themselves have to do with planes.

The 2:00 P.M. refuelling goes badly. It's a clear day with little wind but the two planes can't seem to hang together. Grace misses the canvas bag at first and Willa has to send the Moth into a dive to avoid the bag knocking into the wings. Then the refuelling plane drops too close to the *Adventure Girl*, hovering only fifteen or so feet above it, dangerously close to rolling a wing-tip and shearing off part of the smaller biplane. When Grace finally manages to get the refuelling hose into the empty tank, the refuelling plane doesn't shut the fuel supply off fast enough and the tank overflows and splashes gasoline onto Grace's face and chest. She has to flush her eyes with a bottle of their water and change her shirt. It's one ordeal from beginning to end and brings home the lesson of how lucky they've been so far in their refuelling contacts and how easily something could turn into disaster.

Grace pumps oil up into the crankcase, as she does after each refuelling, and then she tends to her gasoline-soaked shirt, rinsing it through and pinning it to her windshield with hairpins. She combs water through her red hair.

They fly low over the harbour, Willa at the controls. The sun is on its downward arc. A cloud of gulls rises up from the lake below them. Willa sees the large Crosse & Blackwell factory at the corner of Bathurst and Fleet, the nearby Tip Top Tailors building with its name standing in big letters on the roof. As they pass over the shipping channel on the east side of the harbour in the port lands, Willa sees a long line, an *S* bend, in front of the Dominion Boxboard factory. Men looking for work. Seen from the air they are just a pattern shaping the bare earth around the large brick building. She can't see their faces, can't see that look she has become so accustomed to seeing in the faces of men with no work, a mixture of resignation, anger and a little bit of hope. It's always the hope that makes her turn her head away, feel guilty for her job at the Air Harbour, for the fact that only people with money can afford flying lessons. Compared to the daily humiliations and sufferings of families with no work and no money, flying seems a frivolous extravagance. But people like Grace O'Gorman have never been more popular than now, in the worst year so far of the Depression. The more dismal things get, the more people seem to want to believe in the possibility of individual triumph, and the more it is promoted as something to aspire to. Willa looks down at the line of men outside the factory and knows that, no matter what her sympathies, this is the real distance between her world and theirs, this towering wall of air between the plane and the ground.

THE WOMAN across from Del sits bolt upright, doesn't move. It's always women, thinks Del, taking the customer's offered scarf in her hands and squeezing it. It's always women who want to know the future. Del looks up at the grim expression on the woman's face, lips pushed together like an uneven seam of scar tissue. No, she thinks, women want to know what's going to happen to them. What bad things are going to happen to them.

There are times when Del is afraid of what she does. She can feel what is expected of her, feels it radiating over her small table, filling the cramped booth. Say this. Make it make sense. Just say this. And sometimes, on days when knowing the future is no comfort at all, she will shape what she sees into something that resembles her customer's wish. She doesn't want to tell them more bad news. She knows that the people who come to see her are people who are looking for the Fates to crash through into their lives and change them. Happy people have no need of a future.

Del squeezes the woman's worn scarf and closes her eyes. A candle flickers in a darkened room. She sees the edge of something dimly, a bed near a window.

"Someone in your family is sick," she says, her eyes still closed.

She hears the woman opposite her draw her breath in sharply. "My sister," she says in a soft hiss.

Del wraps the scarf around her fist, thinks briefly of Simon and how he wraps his hands before a fight, layers and layers of white, lacy gauze. No good way to tell this woman what she sees. "You'll be asked to do something," she says. "By your sister. You will have to decide something that is almost impossible to decide."

There is silence. The woman hasn't asked the question that everyone asks. Del looks up. "Think about what you can live with," she says. "Afterwards."

Say this. Forgive her. Save her.

Outside the wooden hut the rides click like beads on a wire. Abacus.

The woman reaches across for her scarf, her hands flutter above the candle. "She's already asked me," she says. "To help her die before she gets so awful sick that her mind will be going to rot."

"What have you said?"

"I said I'd come ask you."

After the woman has left, Del goes outside to have a cigarette. She tosses the lit match to the earth and gratefully breathes in the heady tobacco smoke. Her hands are shaking. It is so hard to do this sometimes, to be expected to fix people's lives, to expect it herself. She walks around the side of the hut. There's a man standing there, smoking. He looks over at her and then looks away.

"You're here for your fortune?" Del recognizes the nervousness.

"Yeah, maybe." He looks up again and she sees the lines around his eyes, the strong chin. You used to be handsome, she thinks.

"You look tired," he says.

"So do you."

They both smile. The plane with the women pilots flies overhead and they glance up at the noise and then back at each other.

"Finish your cigarette," he says. "I can wait."

Jack and Del sit opposite each other inside the hut. Del holds onto Jack's wallet, the leather smooth and warm in her hand.

"You're going somewhere," she says.

"I am?" Jack sounds so surprised that, for an instant, Del thinks she is wrong. She squeezes the wallet hard. "Yes," she says. "You're going away. Somewhere you've never been." She stops. Something hot flushes through her skin and makes her feel queasy. "I see you in a kind of hat."

"A hat?" Jack can't make any sense of what this woman is saying. It doesn't seem to be about him at all. What's so mysterious about a hat? Maybe he shouldn't have come. "I have lots of hats," he says.

"No, no." Del concentrates on what she sees in her mind. "A hat. A coat. It's a uniform. You're a soldier, but not on the ground. You're a pilot."

"I *am* a pilot." Jack leans forward and touches Del on the arm. He feels now from her what he sometimes feels with

Grace, that she knows how to save him, knows what it is he should be doing. *Grace.*

"I'm sorry," he says.

"It's all right," says Del. "It's all right." She has seen a glimpse of something that terrifies her and she doesn't know how to ignore it, how to push it back inside her mind and forget she conjured it up from its sleeping state. "There's going to be a war," she says. "A war that will change everything."

"And I'm going." Jack is almost resigned to it now. It starts to feel a bit like a relief that he will have something of his own to do, something that won't be about Grace.

"You're going." His hand is still on Del's arm and she can feel his fingers against her skin. She waits for him to ask the question they can both feel in the space between them, but he doesn't say it.

Am I coming back?

Del sits on the wooden edge watching Rose skewer through the pool, knowing, from habit, the names of the moves Rose makes in the water. Kip. Torpedo. Marching on Water.

The moon rolls across the dark surface. Del's cigarette glows like an old wish in the humid, late-night air.

"Hey there," says Rose, hoisting herself out of the pool to sit beside Del, her legs hanging over the edge into the water.

There's the weak crackle of a plane overhead.

Rose kicks her feet a little. "I'm thinking about doing a show on those girls in the sky." She leans back on her elbows.

Del can smell the cool, metallic odour of her skin. "I could use the high tower," says Rose, her head back. "Swoop down into the water like a plane. I could dress in aviatrix clothes. I've always liked those leather helmets." She looks over at Del. "That could be you and me up there."

Del smiles. "You wouldn't be able to keep still for nine days," she says.

"Air is water," says Rose.

The empty building takes their words and bats them from corner to corner up in the raftered ceiling. They speak and their voices decorate the air.

"I would dress like a pilot," continues Rose. "But I would behave like a plane. Watch. I've been making it up." She lowers herself back into the water and pushes gently away from the side of the pool.

Del smokes her cigarette, watches her friend tell her watery story. She still feels shaky from talking to that pilot, from thinking about the horror of another war. But outside, for now, the world is quiet and sleeping. Just those girls in the plane, guardians of the night sky. She finds comfort in their circling watch over the earth. She finds comfort in their underwater ballet that Rose bends from the water of the pool.

Pendulum.

Propeller.

Tailspin.

When Del gets home Fram is still up, sitting with a beer at the kitchen table. The house is silent. Del pours herself a glass of water, kisses her husband's head as she passes behind him, and then sits down in the chair beside his. She wants to tell him about what she saw when that pilot came into her hut but she knows it would confirm what he's already so sure of and she can't do it, can't let him be right. He would want to talk about it all the time, and she would have to imagine, over and over again, what she doesn't want to imagine, what she is afraid to imagine.

"Hello there," she says. "Busy night on the horses?"

"Not really," says Fram. He takes a pull of beer, sets the bottle back down on the wooden table. There are buds of water growing on the glass. "There's beans if you're wanting something."

"Not hungry." Del traces the etching on the outside of her glass. "Has Simon been by? He was supposed to come to the hut today. Get the goods on that German boy he'll be fighting next."

"He shouldn't be brawling with a German," says Fram. "And you shouldn't be telling him how to fight. It's not your business."

"It's not *your* business," says Del. "Simon and I have always done this. It's the only thing my foretelling is good for these days."

Fram drains his beer bottle, stands up and puts it on the counter. He leans on the wooden board, looking out the small window over the sink. Del sits behind him at the table.

"There's trouble enough with that Swastika Club," he says. "Simon should not be fighting a German. It does no good."

Del hears the plane pass near their house, flying south over the bar. She thinks of Rose. *That could be you and me up there.*

"Simon can look out for himself."

"He shouldn't be making trouble."

"Fram, leave it be." Del turns to him but he's still looking out the window, leaning heavily on the counter.

"Should never have come here," he says quietly. "This country with the Depression and everyone out of work."

"You have work," says Del.

"For how much longer? Now that Sunnyside is up and running, how much longer will Hanlan's be around? There's not room in this end of the city for two amusement parks."

"Well," says Del, "why did you come here, then?" She has only ever lived in one place, this city, can't fully sympathize with Fram's nostalgia for the country he left a full fifteen years ago.

Fram turns around and looks at his wife. "I thought it would be better here," he says. "Isn't that why anyone goes anywhere? They think it will be better than where they are."

"And isn't it?" Del means herself and Maddy, their home, the life they've made together.

"I'm not sure," he says. "I'm not sure that it is."

Tᴴᴇʏ sᴇᴇ ᴛʜᴇ sᴡᴀsᴛɪᴋᴀs at 6:30 in the morning, flying low over Sunnyside to watch the schooner sway at its anchor. Willa is at the controls while Grace peels herself an orange from the breakfast bag. At first Willa's not sure what the small black sign is on the old concrete pier, the remains of a high-voltage hydro tower in the water just east of the girls' softball stadium. She pushes the nose of the plane down on the next circle over the harbour and sees not one, but five painted swastika symbols — the first one on the tower she'd previously spotted and four more on another tower to the southwest of the bathing pavilion. The concrete towers are pyramid shaped and Willa knows from being on the beach near them that they are about fifteen feet high, the tops still pierced with the steel rods that had connected the supports to the rest of the structure, the wands of metal looking like candles on a cake. If the towers are fifteen feet tall, then the painted swastikas are two to three feet in height.

Willa taps Grace on the shoulder, points down over the side of the plane.

They circle twice more over the concrete towers, each time flying lower than the time before. There are no clues closer to the earth. The beach is empty at this time in the morning.

There's nothing else around the area, no more signs or words painted onto the walls of the pavilion or the side of the *Lyman M. Davis*. Nothing written or lying in the sand.

The Sunnyside amusements are open until midnight, so the painting would have to have been done after that. In the dark heart of the night Willa has been used to thinking that the world below belongs to her and Grace, that after the last star of headlight has twinkled home along the Lakeshore, the flat black of the city surrenders its care to the waking heavens. The pulse of the plane in the sky. To think that while they paced the clouds and watched the sleeping earth, someone, in a boat or standing in the shallow water off the beach, painted the Nazi emblems in deliberate brush strokes, in symmetrical patterns on the two concrete pillars.

Grace, swivelled around in her seat, makes the sign for *blue* — the word for *water* followed by the one for *colour*, two closed fists, palms up, opening into spread fingers, the two baby fingers touching at the tips. She reaches over and tugs hard at Willa's collar.

Blue shirts.

The Swastika Club.

Willa had read the papers in July, the stories of uniformed Canadian Nazis patrolling the beaches at the other end of the city. She even remembers an ad for recruitment into the Swastika Club, the boast that they had eighty thousand members country-wide. She knows from Simon Kahane the effect they have on the Jewish population of Toronto, knows too that the chrome badge the members of the club wear costs more than a pound of butter or ten pounds of potatoes.

What will happen, Willa thinks, when the city wakes up, when people discover the vandalism? She can only imagine the reaction, the headlines in the papers. "Swastikas at Sunnyside." She thinks of Simon, tightens her hand into a fist, just as he taught her to do.

In the middle of the day, their tenth in the air, after the 2:00 P.M. refuelling, they develop engine trouble. Grace is flying the last fifteen minutes of her rotation when the engine misfires. They are so used to the steady vibrating drone of the Moth that the break in the rhythm stalls their hearts as well. Willa clutches the sides of her cockpit as the engine coughs. For one awful moment it makes no sound at all and there's just the whine of the wind in the rigging wires. Grace gives the throttle a nudge forward and the Moth sputters and kicks back into life.

Spark plug.

They seem to be running on all cylinders again, but if a spark plug is fouling, it could just be a matter of time before one of the cylinders goes completely. If this happens, then they are in real trouble. A dead cylinder, instead of burning the oil and gas that feeds into it, will spew it out and the propeller will carry it back into their faces. In a monoplane this would be a hazard because it would smear the windscreen and make it difficult to see, but in an open-cockpit biplane this will be utterly fatal. They have nothing to protect themselves from such an occurrence and because the Moth's engine is exposed and directly behind the propeller, they are in a prime target position if it chooses to spray them suddenly. If they are faced with a dead cylinder, they will have no choice but to land the plane and end the flight.

And this happening when Willa has finally stopped dreaming about the engine cutting out. Bumping off to sleep with her head back against the fuselage and waking in cold terror with the knowledge that the engine has stopped. The moment it takes for the silence she thinks she hears to translate itself into the unbroken throaty growl of the fully functioning motor.

Willa takes over the controls at three o'clock and gingerly flies the Moth in its slot on the horizon. She is wet from her chill of fear when the engine failed. She looks at the back of Grace O'Gorman. Turn around, she thinks, and Grace does. They stare at each other over the thin strip of metal plane, the flimsy piece of tin fuselage that keeps them up in the air.

Don't let it end, thinks Willa, her eyes locked with Grace's, both of them acutely aware of the slight stutter in the engine's monologue.

I don't want to land.

At night there's a sudden and unexpected meteor shower. Fire in the sky. Sparks shooting across the dark hearth. A trail of light arches in front of the plane's nose and Willa writes words on Grace's back.

Stars are both hot and cool. Light is something spoken.

In the day they have the clipped sign speech of Grace, all function and shapes in the air. At night Willa enjoys the niceties of language. If she goes slowly enough there is a way to say everything. All the *the*'s and *but*'s. A pause between words to show the end of a phrase or thought, to punctuate a sentence. It feels so luxurious at night to have such a thing as a sentence, to be able to write a complete line, to suddenly understand the worthiness of all the small words, so talk doesn't splutter and jerk along like an engine missing a cylinder.

Willa wants to write *and and and* across the warm flesh of Grace's back. The hopeful arc of it. The way it loops out, just like that line of light in the sky, a path that dances between two points, that defines a connection, that says, *Yes, these things can be joined together*.

THE NEXT DAY is warm and cloudy, always looking like rain but never actually raining. There's fruit and cornbread for breakfast and a new newspaper story from Jack. Willa reads it eagerly while she's having her coffee.

> GIRL FLIERS IN TROUBLE
>
> Grace O'Gorman and Willa Briggs, the young women attempting a record-breaking endurance flight over the Toronto harbour, were almost forced down last night when Grace lost consciousness while at the controls. She slumped forward over the stick and sent the plane into a deathly dive towards the cold tomb of Lake Ontario.

Willa tucks the paper between her knees, pours herself some more coffee from her thermos. Will she save the day again? Jack's articles are getting better than her own fantasies. She reads on.

> Only the quick thinking of Willa Briggs saved the girls from certain doom. Reaching over from

her seat in the rear cockpit she managed, with a
strength wrested from fear, to haul Grace off the
stick and to take control of the Moth.

Good for me, thinks Willa. She likes her strength being
"wrested from fear." Jack is getting quite lyrical.

Grace O'Gorman seems to be fully recovered
once more and is blaming the episode on her weak-
ness from a recent attack of appendicitis.

Of course she has to get better by the end of the article or
else the people on earth might get worried and take some
action to check out the facts, ascertain the safety of the
pilots.

Willa waves the paper in front of Grace's face, but she just
shakes her head. Grace has been refusing to read the articles
anymore, ever since she became an erratic illness-stricken
victim. She can't cope with the possible public erosion of her
superhuman image.

He can't continue this, Willa writes on the back of Grace,
but Grace just shakes her head again.

Yes he can.

There are flutters of white on the ground by the C.N.E. and
Willa and Grace shorten their circle and drop five hundred
feet from their altitude to see what's happening.

Tents. Hundreds of white tents just to the west of the Dufferin Gates. The tents are all the same, circular with peaked roofs. Soldiers? Willa can't figure out why there would be soldiers camping out at the Canadian National Exhibition when the armouries are just down the street. Maybe it's visiting soldiers from America or overseas? Willa's father had been a soldier in the Great War and she remembers him telling her that the C.N.E. had been the site of massive troop demobilizations at the end of that war.

There's a lot of activity at the C.N.E. today and Willa and Grace include it in their circuit so they can watch the wooden booths going up on the midway, the flurry of people around the buildings. Even though the exhibition isn't scheduled to open until the twenty-fifth, vendors take the preceding weeks to construct their displays and ready their performances.

Willa likes the heavy majesty of the C.N.E. buildings, the winged statuary on the Princes Gates at the main entrance to the grounds. She recognizes a lot of the structures from the air — Horse Palace, Automotive Building, Art Gallery, Coliseum, Horticultural Building, Manufacturers' Building. Even some of the smaller buildings are distinguishable by their shapes. The *T* of the Women's Building, the *H* of the Industrial and Process Building, the long capital *I* of the Mother's Rest.

The Canadian National Exhibition is an immense collection of buildings and roads, stretching for one and a half miles from the Princes Gates on Fleet Street to the Dominion Gates at the other end of the complex. Its southern side looks right over the lake, with only the sixty-six-foot width of

Boulevard Drive between the buildings and the water. The boat regatta course, next to the marathon swim one of the most popular features of the C.N.E., runs alongside the road and is visible from the great lawns of the stately stone-and-glass exhibition buildings. It is on Boulevard Drive that Willa and Grace are to land the Moth on August 25, the opening day of the C.N.E.

What Willa has always liked about the C.N.E. is the way it feels like a city, self-contained and self-sufficient. The network of roads within the grounds, all with names and signs — Dominion Street, Hutton Road, Baden-Powell. The diversity of the buildings, everything from an old settler's log cabin to the cairn marking the site of the French Fort Rouille, to the modern building for dogs and cats. Anything one could want or imagine could be found within the grounds of the C.N.E.

They fly over the huge oval of the grandstand and racetrack where in 1917 the famous American aviatrix Ruth Law raced her biplane against a car driven by Gaston Chevrolet around the dirt racetrack. The car won.

Now every year there is a different "Grand Spectacle" performed within the gigantic interior of the oval. This August the play is to be *Montezuma — Dramatic Spectacle of the Spanish Conquest of Mexico*, complete with a huge constructed palace and fireworks finale. Willa has read the publicity posters. She knows that the small undulations in the centre of the racetrack are man-made mountains where actors will swarm up and down in their enthusiastic search for dancing and fighting.

On the morning of August 11 there are no human sacrifices or marauding Spaniards, just high-wire artists practising for their afternoon shows in the grandstand, six people on a wire that Willa can't even see from above. From where she looks down over the side of the plane the six people appear to be treading gingerly on the air alone. Around the perimeter of the racetrack two horses pull a covered wagon.

It's too bad, thinks Willa, that they'll be down before *Montezuma* begins. It would be a thrill to fly through the fireworks. To have all that colour and light exploding in patterns around the plane.

Willa sees all the activity on the small strip of road beside the Grand Spectacle arena as scaffolding and wood transform the bit of grey road into the facades of rides and games-of-chance. If the engine in the plane weren't so loud, she is sure she'd be able to hear the knocking of a thousand hammers, the rough rasp of a thousand saws.

It is surprising that so many people continue to come to the exhibition, and this, 1933, said to be the worst year of the Depression. Last year attendance was up and the same is predicted for this year. People with no jobs coming to spend what little money they have on a ride on the Ferris wheel or a music concert at the Band Stand.

And why not, thinks Willa. If she weren't making such a dramatic entrance into the exhibition and becoming the opening-day event, she would be lining up with the rest of them at the Princes Gates. She'd be eating hot dogs and guessing the weight of the fat lady and watching the swine judging. She'd be looking in the World's Smallest Home of the dwarfs and lining up to peer in the tank at the Giant Man-Killing Octopus. She'd be living, for one day, in the protected happy temporary city of the C.N.E.

From the air the industrious flurry of people and the solid knobs of buildings are comforting. They fly over the construction at the midway and several people even look up and wave to them.

Lower, writes Willa and Grace skims the copper cupola of the Ontario Government Building, the sloped wooden roof of the grandstand. They fly over two women swinging towards each other on two separate trapeze bars. They flip into space, arms and wrists stiff, bodies swaying as a hook in the air.

They fly over the fountain, the rail track and siding on the north border of the grounds. They fly over the five glass greenhouses by the Dominion Gates. The rose garden stains the earth a blood red. From the air it's all one wash of red, scarlet button on a tunic of green.

MADDY SEES the boy walking slowly along the boardwalk towards Ward's Island. It's the same boy she talked to that day at the working boys' camp. She circles him on her bicycle, notes that he carries the wooden model plane in his arms, walking along watching the ground so that he won't trip.

"Where are you going?" says Maddy, riding around him again. She looks at the carefully painted identification numbers on the upper wings of the Moth.

The boy looks up. "Oh," he says, "it's you again."

"Where are you going?"

Maddy makes a wide circle around him. There's the squeak of her pedals turning on their metal stems. The wing-beats of gulls above their heads.

"Mainland. The exhibition. I'm taking my plane over to enter it in the contest." The boy looks up at her again, this time for longer. He almost smiles. "You know," he says, "you were right about those wings. Three and a half inches."

"Of course I was right."

The boy lowers his head and Maddy feels heat rise to her face. She's talking to him as she talks to Miro and she knows that it's not working. She hasn't seen any other children for so long that she's forgotten what to say to them, what words to use. She was never that good at it anyway. In school, most of the other children are afraid of her rabid intensity, and the ones who aren't don't like her for being Jewish. She doesn't have any real friends her own age. She always pretends it doesn't matter but this morning, bicycling alongside this boy on the boardwalk, she aches with being lonely for company.

"Can I come with you?" she asks.

The boy stops walking and she drops down to straddle her bicycle bar. They stare at each other.

"I won't get in the way," she says.

"What about your folks?"

"They work in the day. Sometimes Uncle Simon makes me something horrible for dinner but he's busy today training."

"Training?"

"For his fight tomorrow night. He's a boxer."

"Simon Kahane?" The boy's eyes flicker with interest. "He's your uncle? He's my favourite fighter."

Maddy feels her old confidence surge back. "I can tell you lots of stories about his fights," she says. "I near about go to every one. I could tell you amazing things," she says. "On the ferry crossing."

Maddy stands next to the boy, whose name is Sidney, on the ferry deck. She leans over the wooden safety railing to watch the water churn away from the bows, leaving white wrinkles on the blue oily lake. The Ward's Island ferry dock is scudding slowly astern. The Hanlan's Point roller coaster is just visible to the west, big old rickety hill. She turns to Sidney, whose arms still cradle the delicate plane.

"What kind of working boy are you?" she asks.

"Runner," he says curtly. "In a print shop. Look." He twists a hand over towards Maddy and she sees the black etchings on his palm, all his hand lines filled in with dirt. "Ink," he says. "Doesn't come out easy."

Maddy is jealous of his hands. She would like to be a working boy. She could work in the temporary Air Harbour and clean Grace O'Gorman's plane. Tighten all the rigging wires, tune it up just so. *Perfect*, Grace would purr as she climbed into her cockpit.

"Do you like planes?" she asks Sidney.

"I like to make things," he says. "Doesn't matter what they are. Tell me about Kid Kahane."

They land at the city-side Bay Street docks and take the streetcar west to the exhibition grounds. Maddy is excited about the journey, even if the return fare will cost her some of her washing-Miro money. She doesn't often leave the islands in the summer. On Labour Day in September her parents will take her to the C.N.E. *For research*, they always say, so they can look at the newest freak display or game, something they can appropriate for Hanlan's next year. If she's lucky, they will let her ride on the Ferris wheel, so high that she's sure it feels just like a plane, at the top of the arc all the tiny people and the lake unrolling like a bolt of blue cloth to the south. They will eat popcorn and fight the crowds to see the women's marathon swim, to see Rose emerge greased and victorious after ten miles. This year she will be going for her fourth straight win, a new record in the history of the C.N.E. marathon swim.

Maddy has never been to the exhibition before it opened officially. It's liberating to stroll through the great columns of the Princes Gates without having to pay admission. The model airplane contest is being held in the Automotive Building, which is just to the left inside the gates. She walks with Sidney into the building and waits while he asks a man at a desk where to go.

Maddy likes how big all the buildings are at the C.N.E. They seem palaces after the stunted wooden houses on the islands. She tilts her head right back and makes herself dizzy turning around looking at the high ceiling.

"What are you doing?"

Sidney is back and frowning at her. She can tell that now they're at the C.N.E. he wishes he hadn't let her come with him. Maddy is adept at knowing when people don't want her around.

"Nothing," she says, feeling as if she wants to cry. "I'm doing nothing."

Sidney fills out a sheet of paper and leaves his Moth with the man at the desk. Maddy reads part of the form over his shoulder until he turns around and glares at her. "Models need not be capable of flight." Cowards, she thinks. Boys know nothing about real planes. They know nothing about flying. She stands back against a wall and watches a succession of boys with planes in their arms enter the Automotive Building. She recognizes the models of the aircraft. *Jenny*. *Waco*. *Curtiss Robin*. She recognizes wingspans and tail-skids. She knows if the registration numbers have been painted on the right places. She knows it all. She stands back against the cold stone wall, picking at the loose paint with her grubby nails. *Just for boys.* She knows without a doubt that there's no boy in the world who could build a better plane than she could. Dirty, stinking, fish-rot cowards.

Sidney finishes writing out his entry form and she walks with him back outside. She can't even look at him, she hates him so much, focuses instead on the border of trees lining the Grand Boulevard in front of the Automotive Building. They are all the same size. One has a bird's nest tucked into the upper branches. She imagines the springtime fate of the fledglings.

Dead, she thinks bitterly. Most likely eaten by a huge, cruel animal.

"Look," says Sidney. "I'm going over to the Dufferin Gates. There's boy scouts camping outside the grounds and I've got friends there."

"Boys," says Maddy as though she were spitting in the dirt.

"Eight thousand of them," says Sidney. "Guests of the C.N.E. From out of town and all." He starts walking away from her. "You'll be all right to get back?"

Maddy wishes she had a huge metal spear. She'd strike him down right where he stood. "I've been on the ferry more times than you," she retorts.

Sidney shrugs his shoulders. "Okay," he says, and moves off over the lawn of the Electrical Engineering Building.

Maddy watches him until he's gone. He never turns around, not even once.

She wanders through the exhibition, walks along the midway with all the men hammering their stalls together, a shiny lace of nails in their teeth. She walks by the painted facades for the Knife-Throwing Chimpanzee and one for the Plate-Balancing Juggler. She finally climbs up into the empty seats of the grandstand and watches the acrobats practise their trapeze act. One woman flips through the air towards another woman who's upside down. The diving woman has her arms outstretched like wings. Grace O'Gorman's Moth skims the rind of sky above the roof of the grandstand.

One woman hooks into another and they swing back and forth in the sky.

Maddy huddles into her wooden seat, her sobs muffled under the noise of the plane.

NIGHT OF DISASTER
ENDURANCE FLIGHT IN PERIL ONCE AGAIN

The girl pilots faced another setback in their bid to set a new world's record for staying aloft. Eleven days into the attempt aviatrix Grace O'Gorman was knocked overboard and hung upside down, attached to her plane only by her flight harness twisted around her ankle.

The tragedy occurred when the refuelling plane, flown by Grace's husband, Jack, was lowering a bag of fuel tins and food. A sudden gust of wind swung the bag right at the famous flier and knocked her off balance. She toppled from the Moth, her foot luckily catching in her safety harness as she pitched head first over the side of the plane. Willa Briggs could do nothing but watch in horror as her partner plummeted towards her certain fate. With lightning speed Willa sprang to her feet, leaving no one at the controls, and reaching over the side of her cockpit managed to get a hold of Grace's ankle and slowly pull her back into the safety of the plane.

Even for such air-minded girls as Grace and Willa, these dangerous incidents are taking their toll. "We're a bit nervous about what might happen next," says a weary Willa Briggs.

You bet we're nervous, thinks Willa. She tucks the paper down beside her seat. She hopes that her mother isn't reading these articles, and then she hopes that she is. It occurs to Willa that Jack might be planning something. What if all these fabricated stories, with their escalating drama, are merely the preparation for something real? What if he is plotting something that will really end their flight? They are so utterly dependent on his coming to refuel the Moth every eight hours that they are largely under his control. If he does plan on sabotaging them, there won't be much that they could do about it. Willa has never thought Jack calculated enough to be capable of orchestrating a full-scale attack. She's thought that his invented newspaper stories came out of his sense of powerlessness, not out of any sense of careful strategy. What if she's been wrong about his motives? What if she's underestimated him as a potential threat?

Willa looks at the back of Grace. Can she tell this woman that she fears her husband is out to scuttle them? Can she tell Grace that she thinks Jack will betray her? What words can she write on Grace's skin that won't make her flinch and pull away?

The engine of the Moth is still misfiring but it doesn't get any worse. It doesn't cut out like before. There's just the steady tapping of the out-of-sync cylinder.

Willa and Grace spend the twelfth day in the air inventing more signs for their language. It rains a little and the sky is overcast. They sit in their oilskins, just in case, Grace turned in her seat to face Willa, pulling words out of the air.

They have a lot of basic descriptive words, but there's a need to move beyond merely describing individual things. Grace starts combining words to produce another word out of the association. She signals *colour* and then draws an invisible *R* in the air with her forefinger.

Red.

She signals *colour* again and this time traces a Y.

Yellow.

She puts both hands out in front of her, palms up and shifts them up and down like weigh scales, the sign for *equal.*

It takes Willa a moment to make the leap, but when she sees what Grace is doing her mind pounces on the new word eagerly.

Red and Yellow equal Orange.

Grace does a few more colour combinations and then moves on to more difficult matches.

Plane and Boat equal

Vehicles?

Willa has thought that the unifying category for *plane* and *boat* is *vehicle*, but someone else could just as easily think *transportation* or *mechanical things* or even *things not on land.* Grace might not even have meant *vehicle* when she signed *plane* and *boat*. What happens in that space between what is meant and what is taken? If everything is clear and understood, as it was when Willa and Grace communicated in single, solid images, will there be less to say? Is it the tension between one person's intended meaning and the other person's perceived meaning that keeps people talking?

Grace begins signing two words that don't appear to belong to each other but when placed together suggest another word, suggest an answer to the riddle they pose. The combination of *night* and *wing* produces *bat,* and *sky lip* conjures *horizon.* This is a way of producing meaning without actually identifying the subject. Language as a visual echo. A word all the more vivid because it has travelled across other words to arrive at its meaning. A bat floating out of darkness on angel's wings.

Creating a visual resonance for language is not something that happens in written and spoken English and Willa is now starting to realize what a lack this is. She is starting to think that if she can't see, then she won't be able to talk.

The cloudy day gives way to a cloudy night. No stars and the moon shimmering in the sky. They circle the harbour, looking down at the lights of the city, the stars of the ground. It's a calm night, not a lot of wind, and they coast slowly around and around their worn groove in the air. At close on midnight Willa throttles back to forty-five miles per hour. The engine drops out of its own sound and for the moment that it takes for her ear to adjust to the new timbre there's just the perfect notes of the wind plucking the rigging wires.

As they're coming over the city side, flying west above the C.N.E., there's a sudden spurt of brightness from below, a wobble of light in the sky beside them and then huge illuminated patterns in the air. It takes Willa a moment to recognize what they are. Letters, words. A telegram of light.

HELLO GIRLS — KEEP FLYING.

Willa blinks, slaps herself on the side of her face, blinks again. It's still there. Impossibly there are words in the sky. She pokes Grace in the back and Grace reaches over and grabs her hand to hold it still. She's seen it too. Willa's not out of her mind. She tugs the flashlight up from its cord on her neck and shines it into the darkness over the C.N.E. The tube of light from the torch only makes it to the end of the wing.

HELLO GIRLS — KEEP FLYING.

What is happening down on earth? What maniacs are in charge of the planet? How can letters that each look to be about four feet high just appear and hang still in the ether? What is going on?

Willa drops her flashlight and it bangs back hard against her breastbone. She swings the plane out towards the islands, the big illuminated sign in back of them for a minute. When they pull round to the left and Willa looks across the harbour towards the C.N.E., it's gone. No shapes in the darkness. No alphabet of light.

ON SUNDAY, AUGUST 13, it rains all day. Relentless rain, and Willa is convinced that because they are close to the clouds it falls harder on them than it does on earth. They spend the day in oilskins, and underneath they wear all the clothes they can — to keep warm and also to keep the clothes dry. Willa feels as if she's wearing a 150-pound diving suit, just as the young Miss Owens will at the end of the month when she lowers herself into the water of the bay so she can "see what the bottom of the lake looks like."

After the 6:00 A.M. refuelling they climb to four thousand feet and Willa finds it a relief not to have to look at the world below the plane. What's down there is less and less interesting, and especially now when it's all smeared with mist.

Willa tries to drink her coffee without letting the rain into it, but it's impossible. The rain fills her thermos lid. It gets into the breakfast bread and reduces it to a soggy wad of dough. The rain runs down her hair and face, enters her oil-skins at her neck and runs in thin trickles down her chest and down her back. The rain soaks her leather gloves right through and she knows that when she takes off the gloves her hands will be stained brown for days from the dye. The rain makes it hard to see. It drives into her face at an angle because of the forward motion of the plane and it stings against her skin.

The rain does not stop.

The 2:00 P.M. refuelling is difficult. Twice the bundle is lowered towards Grace and twice she can't grab onto it and it bumps across a portion of the upper wing before Jack's plane pulls it up again. When Grace does manage to keep it in the Moth she has problems undoing the bag itself, her hands cold and stiff from the rain, and eventually she just cuts the thin length of rope around the neck of the canvas sack. Willa wishes there were three of them for the refuelling. It's what's needed — two to deal with the hose and the tins of fuel and one to fly the plane. She watches Grace struggle to maintain her balance as she forces the hose into the wing tank. What if she just blew over the side of the plane, could Willa get to her in time? No, she thinks. I wouldn't be the way I am in Jack's stories. I couldn't save Grace. She keeps the Moth as steady as she can. The rain tastes like metal in her mouth.

The bad weather lasts until just before dawn. It takes Willa a moment to realize that it's not raining, she's so used to the constant rinse of water on her face that when she finally notices that it's not coursing down her body any more she has no idea if it's been moments or hours. Grace is curled into a yellow ball in the front cockpit, sleeping in the uncomfortable way they've learned to sleep. Willa points the nose of the plane into the circle of red that's hoisting itself out of the lake, as though she can help raise it up high enough to feel its heat enter her cold, cold bones.

It's just after 5:00 A.M. and the world is still dark, washed with grey and shadow. The spark plug wires have shed voltage in the damp and there's a halo glowing around the engine. St. Elmo's fire. Good old plane, thinks Willa. All that rain and it never faltered once. Water is a danger to an exposed engine like the Moth's; the magneto could get wet and short the engine out. Water and electricity aren't a good mix. Willa looks at the halo. It's almost as if the Moth was aware of them — not human, but conscious somehow of who they are and what they are doing. As if it knows how important it is for everything to run smoothly.

Two weeks, thinks Willa. Today's the fourteenth day. Two weeks in the air.

She'll have to wake Grace up soon so they can get ready for the 6:00 A.M. refuelling. It's as though that's how they mark time, the day dividing neatly into the three sections between refuelling bouts. Willa can see the hunch of Grace's shoulders, her head tipped forward onto her chest.

Grace.

I want to stay up here with you forever.

Two weeks and Willa thinks she feels better than ever. Of course she has trouble remembering what she felt like a few days ago, but she's not concerned about that. She doesn't feel so tired any more, though something tells her that she is really more tired than ever and this is just some kind of reaction to exhaustion, this nervous kind of elation. But it's all right. This is what she says to herself all the time. It's all right that her feet feel permanently numb. It's all right that she has no real appetite lately. It's all right that twice she's seen things that weren't there — other planes coming towards them out of the dark. It's all right. She tosses that two-word chant from side to side in her head, catching it, throwing it, catching it, throwing it.

It feels as if each rotation of the plane around the harbour pulls the red sun a little higher out of the water.

Grace sleeps on.

The sun swings a bloody arm across the waves. Willa looks at her hand on the stick, small bone bow at the wrist, flat-back grin of knuckles. It knows what to do by itself, she thinks. Her hand pivots slowly to follow the pull of the north sky.

This way.

That way.

Meridian charmer.

Compass of bone.

D EL WALKS across the grounds of the amusement park. It's a cold night, that storm yesterday washed in a lot of cooler air from somewhere. She pulls her sweater tighter around her shoulders as she passes Miro's bungalow. The light's on. He has trouble sleeping, she knows that. He sits up and listens to the radiogram, reads his boys' adventure annuals. Tales of mountain climbs and solo ocean voyages. Tales of flight.

Rock. Water. Air.

Del hears the plane, looks up but can't see anything. It sounds higher up tonight, far away. The sky leaks starlight. Over the C.N.E. she can see the big lit-up words of greeting to the pilots.

WE SALUTE YOU GIRLS.

Skyogram. A British invention, imported for the exhibition and tested with those nightly messages to the pilots. Everyone was excited about the skyogram. A revolutionary idea, to project letters onto a giant tethered balloon that floated above the grounds of the C.N.E. Even the islanders were interested in this one. It was one thing that happened on the mainland that they could actually participate in. Del just wishes they'd think of something better to say to Grace O'Gorman and Willa Briggs. Something that might be interesting to them. Maybe that's why they're flying so high tonight, to escape the insipid salutations.

A chill wind comes twisting through the wooden supports of the Dips and Del hurries on towards the protection of her booth. One more hour and then she'll go home. It's a slow night at the amusement park, too cold for people to come across the bay. Fram is slow too. She left him with no customers at the carousel, just Maddy riding round and round on the horses and Fram watching her.

It's warmer inside the tiny booth; the curtained entranceway blocks the draft. Del lights two candles and settles herself down behind the small table. She ties what she thinks of as "the gypsy scarf" around her head, and just as she's tightening the knot at the back someone comes into the hut.

A young man. He grins at her and sits right down on the stool, doesn't wait for her to tell him what to do.

Confident, thinks Del. She lowers her hands from her head, puts them down on the table in front of her.

"Do you want your fortune told?" she asks.

The man leans over the table, still grinning, pushing his face right up near hers.

Del's breath catches in her throat.

"No," he says. "I'll be telling *your* fortune, Jew bitch." He stands up suddenly, knocking over the table and grabbing her by the shoulders. Del can now hear the stamping of feet beyond the walls of the hut as she's pulled by the man through the curtain and outside. There's a whole group of them around her booth. Young men in blue shirts. Swastika Club.

"Here she is," says the man who's dragged her outside. "It's his sister." He throws her into the arms of one of the blue shirts and she's pushed from man to man around the perimeter of her booth. They are rough with her, shoving her along hard. One of them slaps her across the face with the back of his hand and Del feels the thick stickiness of blood pool inside her mouth.

"Tell your brother he shouldn't have won that fight against Peter Reiter," says the man who hit her and then Del understands what this is all about. Simon beat a German on Saturday night, beat him handsomely, had the blond boy bleeding on the ropes after the third round.

Del is pushed faster and faster around the circle of men. She sees the blur of raised hands, the flat blue sea of their chests. She hears torn bits of speech. "Watch for the signs." "Deserve justice." She falls and someone kicks her in the stomach. She curls around the pain, waiting for the other blows. But when she opens her eyes she sees that the mass of men have moved away from her. They're clustered around her booth and she smells the match before she sees it, crawls on her stomach a few yards and collapses. Her booth is over on its back. There's a small gasp of flame around the base. Bigger now. The men are yelling something she can't make out. They're kicking at the flimsy wood of the hut as it burns. From the ground Del can see the shine of their boots as they raise and lower through the flame. She can see the glint of orange in the tin cut-outs of the stars and moon that she had nailed to the outside walls of the booth. And far up in the night sky, as she lies bleeding into the cold earth, she can see the huge illuminated words over the C.N.E.

WE SALUTE YOU GIRLS.

Maddy sees the flames as she's passing Miro's house. Something is burning in the middle of the amusement park. Usually the bonfires are near the water, not in the middle of buildings. Usually they're on weekends. She hurries forward and then stops quickly. She sees the ring of men around the fire, their faces smudged with greasy light. She sees the shape of what's burning: a rectangle. Something winks like a star through the dark.

Maddy opens her mouth but nothing comes out. She sees the outline of someone lying on the ground, a little behind the group of men. It's her mother. Del lies on her side, knees drawn up to her chest. One arm curls protectively around her head. She doesn't move. Maddy's heart lurches in her ribs like an animal hurling itself against the bars of a cage.

Overhead there's the dim whir of the Moth. The sound breaks through to Maddy and she turns and runs for her father, underneath the comforting, familiar noise of the plane.

THE WIND JOSTLES the Moth. All day a wind so strong that Willa can watch the wings shake, the rigging wires pull back like bowstrings. She thinks that wind is worse than rain, that it's the worst of anything. All the noise, the roar around her head, the force of the slipstream like a hand constantly pushing her away. The way it moans in hollow vowels, always on the edge of saying something but never getting there. It's the noise that makes her feel like jumping overboard into the lake to drown out the awful cacophony of almost-voices.

At least the temperature's warmer than yesterday and the wind doesn't drive a chill into her. At least there's that. Willa scrunches down under her small windscreen.

It's the fifteenth day. Grace is flying the plane. They've just had a bad 2:00 P.M. refuelling, the hose jerking out of Grace's hands and spraying her with gasoline, one of the empty fuel tins blowing over the side.

It's the last half-hour of Grace's flying shift.

Willa curls around the stick, feels it move ever so slightly left as Grace banks them over the port lands. She has her hands over her ears. That's better. She likes feeling the pressure of the stick against her stomach as Grace controls the

Moth. It's as if Grace is pulling her left over the city skyline, as if Grace is controlling her.

There's some orange peel on the floor of the cockpit and a pencil stub rolling around the dirty sheet metal. From when we used to write, thinks Willa. She picks it up and examines it as though it were a million-year-old fossil or a piece of debris from outer space. Pencil. Plain wood, the lead rounded at the tip. Maybe two and a half inches long. She pushes the point into her cheek and feels the hard tip with her tongue, the pencil making her cheek concave, pushing it inside out.

Tucked down beside Willa's head, in the space between the seat and the side of the cockpit, is the latest newspaper story from Jack. Willa hasn't read it yet, doesn't feel up to her documented heroics today. Still lying in a foetal position she pulls the paper out from where it's wedged and lays it on the floor of the cockpit. With the pencil she draws a few tentative lines on the newsprint. They used to write notes to each other, she remembers that, but she has no idea of what they used to say. It feels strange to hold a pencil again. The way they talk now is immediate, isn't mediated through paper and pencil, through any kind of distance. It happens on skin, in the air, their bodies signalling and responding. This is what talking is and the desire now is for this new expression, for a language that lives in the body.

Grace.

The stick pushes against her ribcage and her breath unravels.

The thing she wants to say to Grace is a thing she's afraid to tell her. Afraid that if she spells it out on Grace's smooth, warm skin, Grace will pull away from the words. It is both the most simple and the most complicated thing she's ever wanted to say to someone else and the more she doesn't say it, the more it bangs against the inside of her head, trying to get out.

Willa pulls the pencil in thick, repeated strokes overtop the latest story about the *Adventure Girl* flight, the latest lie from Jack.

I love you.

It scares her to see it, the soft pencil lines bold and readable over the black type of the story.

"ADVENTURE GIRLS" ENTER THIRD WEEK ALOFT.

I love you.

Willa adds a word underneath the line.

Grace.

She looks up from the floor of the cockpit, sees the instrument panel and above that the fingernail of windscreen, sees an arm up in the air. It's her turn to fly the plane. Willa scrabbles back into a sitting position, pushes her feet into the rudder channels and takes the stick in her right hand. Her left hand still holds onto the newspaper. Grace, feeling the pressure on the stick, puts her hand down and turns around in her seat. Her blue eyes are dull with fatigue, but even tired she looks like a million bucks, thinks Willa.

Grace smiles and it's as though the smile tugs Willa's left arm up and extends the newspaper over the strip of fuselage between the two cockpits. The wind flaps the flimsy newsprint, tries to tear it from her hands. Grace doesn't look down. She smiles at Willa and Willa smiles back and the plane flies itself over the islands. And Willa suddenly knows, from the shadows in Grace's eyes, from the twang of the rigging wires as the wind drags its fingers through them, that Grace doesn't feel the same way she does. Grace doesn't love her back.

Under the unrelenting pounding of the wind and engine, Willa can hear the beating of her own heart in her chest. She opens her left hand and the newspaper parachutes backwards over the rear of the plane and disappears.

MADDY STANDS beside her mother's bed. The afternoon light levels in the window and dust particles float above the bedcovers where Del lies wedged up by pillows. Downstairs Maddy can hear the bang and clang of her father fixing dinner — cupboards opening and closing, pots unseated from their shelves and each other. She stands absolutely still, wishing herself away from this room, looking over her mother's pale hands on top of the sheets to the dust riding the corridor of light from the window.

Del did not break, she bruised. Fram had run back to the booth with Maddy, holding her hand too tightly all the way and not speaking. But when they got there the blue shirts had left, people were putting out the fire and tending to Del. The booth was ruined, all skeleton and ash.

Del did not break. The doctor came and poked at her. He sighed a lot and lifted her arms up and down. She said *yes* and *not really* and *only if I move this way* to his prodding and his questions. Del did not cry. A policeman came and took a statement. *They all looked the same, it was the uniform.* He licked his lips and turned the pages of his black notebook. *I don't know how tall they were.* He didn't stay as long as the doctor. The buttons on his jacket were shiny.

Del lies in bed, where she's been for almost one whole day. Fram had Jim mind the carousel so he could stay with her. All day he's probably been fussing about, bringing her things and asking how she is. Maddy's been out on her bicycle since early morning, but now that she's back Fram has made her come upstairs. *Your mother's been asking for you. Go on and see her.*

Del smiles up at Maddy. Her hair looks so dark against the blanch of the pillows.

"Hey there," she says, and Maddy feels her throat squeeze in on itself. She curls her hands into fists.

Del pats the edge of the bed. "Come sit by me."

Maddy shakes her head.

There's the thump of a pot going on the stove from downstairs.

"What's your father making for our supper?"

"Don't know."

"I'm all right," says Del. "Nothing broken. I'll be up and out of bed by tomorrow or the day after. It's only a precaution. They didn't hurt me. It was more the shock than anything."

You're lying, thinks Maddy. She hasn't told her mother that she was there, that she saw the fire and the men and Del on the ground.

The sun through the window makes Del look ghostly, makes her look sick.

"Why didn't you know?" asks Maddy. "Why couldn't you tell your own future?"

Del looks down at her hands on top of the bedclothes. There's a long scratch on the back of her left hand. Someone's ring, she thinks. One of them must have had a ring. There's a cut like that on her cheek from where one of them hit her across the face with the back of his hand.

She remembers the man coming into her booth. How confident he seemed. But that was all. Confident. She'd had none of the feelings she usually had with clients, no turning a dark corner in her mind and seeing a scene in a room. No woman being passed from man to man. No fire and the taste of blood and fear in her mouth. The young man was *confident*, that's all she knows.

"It doesn't work for me," she says. "The future, I mean. I can only see it for other people."

———

Maddy sits at the kitchen table. Her father ladles soup into the bowl in front of her. Weak-looking broth, sullen lumps of carrot and onions, lardy potatoes.

"No one has soup in the summer," she says, picking up her spoon and stirring around the mess in her bowl to make a whirlpool.

"We do," says Fram. He sits opposite her and sucks the broth noisily off his spoon.

Maddy imagines her mother eating her bowl of soup upstairs in the bedroom, carefully spooning the vegetables to her swollen lips, trying not to spill on the sheets.

"I'm not going up there again," she says. "To see her."

Fram puts down his spoon. The look he gives Maddy over the top of his bowl almost makes her cringe. "You stop blaming your mother," he says. "I know you're upset, but what happened, happened to *her*. It was an act of hatred and stupidity."

"Because she's Jewish," says Maddy, her face filling up with the feeling of anger. "They beat her up because she's a dirty Jew. They burned down the little house." She feels tears kicking at the corners of her eyes and swipes savagely at them with her hands, before they drop to the table, before Fram sees that she's crying.

"Girl," says Fram, softer now, "if anyone's to blame, it's Simon. They came to revenge the German boy he fought on Saturday. Your mother was a way for them to be getting at Simon."

"Because she's Jewish," says Maddy, her voice a raw whisper in the still of the room. "Say it, Dad. Don't lie. I was there and I saw what they did. *I was there.*"

Fram's voice is steady as the low foghorn out on the bay. "Yes," he says. "Because she's Jewish."

"**H**ELLO, DEL."

Del opens her eyes to see Rose sitting on the edge of her bed. The soft twilight from the window makes her look faintly luminous as she perches on the mattress as if she's sitting on a straight-backed chair. Uncomfortable, thinks Del. She's less sure of herself on dry land.

Mermaid.

"Rose," she says. "I didn't hear you come in."

"I'm between shows," says Rose. She lifts her leg slightly so that Del can see the jodhpurs and boots that she wears. "Aviatrix," she says. "The crowd goes wild for it. My matinee was sold out."

Del smiles and it hurts her face. "Propeller," she says.

Rose smiles back. "Tailspin."

A breeze from the open window ruffles Rose's baggy white shirt. Del can't remember the last time she saw her friend in actual clothes. She looks older than she seems in the water. Same as me, thinks Del. Thirty-five.

"You look good," she says, which isn't true and the wind pushing the ruck of sheet above her seems to be her breath, gone from her body.

"You don't," says Rose. They laugh and it is easy again.

"Seriously." Rose leans forward, puts a hand on Del's shoulder. "When I heard, there was a man running around, all excited. Know what he was saying?"

Del shakes her head.

"'They beat up a Jew. They got a Jew.'" Rose pushes away from Del's shoulder as though she's pushing off from a wall, sliding out to the safer dark of the pool. "It was you."

"It was me," says Del.

"And I didn't do anything."

"You didn't know."

"And *you* didn't know."

"I can't," says Del. "I can't foretell my own life. That's the way it goes in my line of work."

"Well," says Rose, "that's not very helpful, is it?"

Del has often thought so herself. And the truth is, she thinks, inching her body up to a better position on the pillows, the truth is that if she couldn't tell fortunes, she wouldn't. She does it because she can, runs her whole life like that. Sometimes it gets hard to distinguish what she wants from what she is capable of having.

"And," says Rose, "on top of the scare with you, I heard from my mother, finally." She fishes a letter out of her breast pocket and holds it out towards Del. "She's in a panic. They've taken my father away. Detained him. She doesn't know what is going on. They won't let her see him and she's hopeless unless he's telling her what to do."

Rose runs a hand through her hair, turns to the splash of air from the window, the sound of the plane in the sky. "I thought I'd better go over and see what's happening. It sounds as if he's been arrested but there's no real charge. Or they won't tell my mother. Or she's got it wrong. Anyway."

Rose turns again to Del.

"He's an old man. There's no one else to do it. I thought I'd wait until after the race though. It's not long now and I just can't pass up my chance at a fourth straight win. Selfish I know, but I want the record. I want to be written up in history. But I can go right after that. Next day even."

Del holds the letter in her hand, doesn't take it from the envelope. She can feel heat searing through her flesh. She can see the shadow edge of something, a wall, a room. Some kind of dormitory.

"Don't go," she says. This is it, she thinks. No matter how much she wants to turn from it sometimes, she can't. This is what her life is for. To save the ones she loves. "You'll win the swim. That's all right, but don't go back to Germany."

Rose looks skeptically at her friend. "Don't try that on me, Del," she says. "I'm not one of your worried widows."

"Oh no," says Del. "I have to scare you. So you don't go."

"Del."

It's not a question or a plea but there's something of both in the way she says it. Also apprehension. Also reprimand.

"You can't," warns Del. "You have to believe me."

"I don't have to," says Rose.

She shifts on the edge of the bed. There's the creak of the mattress, a shimmer of birdsong from outside.

"You're asking me to choose."

"No I'm not," says Del. "I'm asking you to trust me." Del

drops the letter and grabs both of Rose's hands in hers. She can smell the pool on Rose's skin.

"Rose," she says. "It's me talking. It's me here."

During the 6:00 a.m. refuelling on the sixteenth day there's an accident. It's first light and Grace is standing in her cockpit waiting to catch the canvas bag that drops from the open cabin door of the monoplane. This is always the most nerve-racking part, the point just before contact, before the length of rope and hose draws a line between the two planes and connects them.

Willa flies by feel, keeping her eyes constantly on the underside of the refuelling plane, trying to fit her speed and altitude to its movements. Every day it seems to get harder to be so precise in these sky patterns.

Grace, standing braced in her cockpit, has just put her arms up to receive the bundle of supplies when there's a sudden swat of wind and the Moth gets knocked slightly sideways. Grace manages to steady herself by holding onto the wing tank, but as she puts her hands down to balance herself this way the bag swings into the plane and tears into a section of the upper wings, ripping the fabric. Grace somehow hauls the bag in before it lifts most of the wing covering off, but damage has been done. As Grace unloads the fuel tins and then positions the fuel hose in the tank, Willa watches the rent in the wing being pecked at by the wind and increasing in size. It doesn't seem that a strut has been broken but something has to be done or the fabric will be completely lifted off and the wings will be too badly damaged to function properly. Willa gauges the distance from the fuselage to the repair site. It's fairly near the wing tank so it should be possible to stand on the base of the lower wing where it touches the body of the plane and lean up and over to reach the rip. They packed a can of dope — a liquid glue-varnish — as part of their equipment. It's stashed in the rear compartment behind Willa's seat. She could use one of her shirts for repair fabric as she doesn't think they have any canvas or patch material.

By the time the refuelling is done Willa has worked out a plan to get to the rent in the wing. Jack, in the monoplane, unaware or unconcerned about what's happened, reels in the rubber piping and his plane lifts up from the thorax of the Moth, its mating ritual completed. When Grace is back down in her seat, after stowing and securing the fuel tins and pumping oil into the engine, Willa taps her on the shoulder to get her attention and make her turn around in her seat.

She points to the rapidly fraying upper wing, the flag of loose fabric flapping in the slipstream. She points to herself. She makes the motion of painting with a brush. Grace nods. She looks exhausted. Every refuelling encounter seems to tire her more than the last. Even though she's supposed to begin her flying shift right after the contact, Willa often has to let her sleep for an hour first now to enable her to get her strength back.

Grace looks sternly at Willa, points over the side of the plane and then grasps the edge of her cockpit firmly with both hands.

It's a long way down. Be careful.

Willa rips the sleeves off her spare white shirt. One of the sleeves she shoves into the space behind her seat. The other she will use as a brush and she pushes it and the rest of the shirt down the front of the shirt she's wearing. The can of dope is under her pile of clothes. She jettisons the lid with a fork. Because she'll have to hold onto the can with one hand, she'll only have one hand to hold onto the plane. She stands up. Grace slows the airspeed of the plane by throttling back. The wind's not as bad as the day before but it's gusty, which makes it potentially more dangerous. Willa undoes the port door of her cockpit and it drops down against the fuselage. She reaches her left hand for the trailing edge of the upper wing and guides her left foot onto the step area of the lower wing. She's half in the plane and half out. They're flying over the water and she can see the wispy white threads of waves. Her legs feel all a-wobble. She pulls on the wing and swings her right leg out of the plane, hooks it around the base of the rigging wires so it can't slide. The wind ratchets up and down her body. I could never be a wing-walker, she thinks and sneaks a look at Grace, beside her but sitting in the plane. Grace is watching the horizon, both hands steady on the stick. Willa puts the can of dope on the shelf of upper wing and reaches for the pieces of shirt that she's tucked down her chest. Carefully she draws them out, spreads the large piece over the ragged hole and stuffs the smaller piece into the can. Dope is extremely sticky and within seconds her hand is covered in the glue and is stuck to the makeshift brush. She smears the liquid over the patch of shirt, adhering it to the smooth unharmed fabric of the wing. It won't be pretty, but as long as she covers every inch of the replacement cloth it should hold.

Stick and cloth, thinks Willa as she plasters the dope over the hole. All that holds us in the sky is a bit of stick and cloth, something infinitely more fragile than the human body itself.

Grace puts a hand on Willa's leg when she's finished patching the wing and guides her foot back into the rear cockpit. Willa's right hand is stuck to the dope can so she doesn't have to worry about dropping it as she gingerly steps backwards to safety. Her right leg buckles when it hits the cockpit floor and she collapses heavily into her seat, the plane rocking in protest. Some of the dope has spilled down her arm and she will spend the rest of the day picking it off. Dope smells and acts like fingernail polish and it has to be peeled off the skin when it hardens.

Made it. Willa pulls up the cockpit door and latches it securely. She's trembling, her legs shaking so much that her heels thrum a rhythm on the cockpit floor. She looks up to where the upper wing is still a wing, doesn't unravel like a pulled strand in a sweater. Her body feels as if it's crackling with a thousand tiny fires.

Grace gives her the thumbs-up sign from the front cockpit. They fly low over the city.

Willa starts to cry.

SIMON TAKES the ice pack from his sister and puts it down on the bed beside him.

"One other time," he says. "Just ten minutes more."

Del puts a hand up to her face and pinches her cheek. "My face is numb, Simon. Numbness seems worse than bruising."

"Swelling," says Simon. "Bruising and swelling."

"Whatever," says Del impatiently. "I'm getting bored with this. I can't sit here all day moving that old towel full of ice over the sore parts of my body."

"Why not?" says Simon. To him it seems easy. He lives his life in three related states — training to fight, fighting, recovering from fighting. They are all full-time satisfying occupations. "You're recovering."

"I'm bored," says Del. "There's things I have to do. My livelihood's been burned down. My daughter won't talk to me. I can't fix anything being a bedridden invalid."

"You're very impatient," says Simon. "I thought you grew out of that."

"Oh shut up," says Del.

She can hear the world outside the house and it's making her restless. The sound of people walking along the bar. The flutter of waves on the beach. Up above the house the tin-throated whine of the plane carrying the two girl pilots around and around the perimeter of the bay.

"Where's Maddy?" she says.

"I don't know." Simon gets up and goes to the window, looks out, his back to Del. "Can't see her. Off on her bike somewhere, I expect. As usual."

"I wish she'd talk to me," says Del. "She blames me for getting hurt, you know."

"Why would she do that?" says Simon. He doesn't turn around, continues watching out the window. "You want me to find the boys, Del?"

"The boys?"

"The blue-shirts. The ones who came and roughed you up."

"No. No more trouble. I just want to get on with things. Simon?"

He turns from the window when she says his name.

"Come and finish with this ice. Then I'd like a pot of tea, maybe some lunch. You could make me a sandwich."

———

Simon sees Maddy bicycling up the street as he's leaving the house. He walks towards her and she comes hurtling in and brakes hard just inches in front of him. She drops down to straddle the crossbar of the bike.

"Where were you?" says Simon impatiently.

"Where was I?" Maddy looks at him, incredulous. "Why would I tell you?"

"Because," says Simon, trying to keep his voice low so that Del won't hear them from up in her room. "Your mother's worried. Why aren't you up there keeping her company?"

"Don't have to," says Maddy.

"She's shaken up," says Simon. "She needs you."

Maddy almost tells him that she was there, that she saw the men and the fire, her mother on the ground, that she felt so afraid her mother was dead and if the men saw her, they would kill her too. Jew-girl. And now it's as if her mother really is dead. Maddy can't go near her, that night turns and turns in her head, pushes Del further and further away from her. And she remembers what her father said, how it's partly Simon's fault for winning the fight against the German.

"I don't have to do anything you tell me," she says fiercely.

Simon reaches down and grabs hold of her handlebars, gives the bike a little shake. "I'm your family. I'm part of where you come from and one day, Maddy Stewart, maybe when you're grown, you'll catch yourself saying things like your father says now, or moving the way your mother does. Or you'll back out of a dream into a waking morning with your fists up and you'll remember how to slip inside on someone and come up with a right hand from below."

Simon leans in close towards her, his head inches from hers.

"And you'll think of me, Maddy Stewart. You won't be able to help it. You'll think of me."

———

Maddy creeps up the stairs to her room, but she's not quiet or fast enough. When she's on the landing just outside her door she hears the tentative voice of her mother.

"Is that you, Maddy?"

From where she stands Maddy can look through the open door of her parents' room and see the lower half of the bed, her mother's legs beached under the sheets like driftwood. Past the bed there's the window, curtains lifting into the room with the breeze, like somebody waving a white handkerchief of distress.

Maddy opens the door to her room, steps inside and closes it behind her. In contrast to her parents' room hers is dark and cluttered, curtains permanently drawn across the one square of window. She wades through the clothes and pieces of wood on the floor, the bent bicycle and buggy wheels — salvage from the bay. There's a small table beside her bed and she stands over it, digs into her pocket and drops a small object into a partitioned box that lies across the surface of the table. The box is an old printer's tray, the wooden interior divided into a multitude of small sections. Some of the sections are full of objects, some are empty. The sections that have an object are backed by a piece of paper with a number printed carefully onto it in pencil. Number ten is an old bolt. Number five is a mouldy apple core. Maddy has deposited a fragment of chicken bone on top of a piece of paper with the number seventeen printed on it. The wooden box is a calendar of found objects from the *Adventure Girl.* August 17 — chicken bones from one of their airborne meals. There are some spaces in the cataloguing, days when Maddy couldn't find anything that could possibly have fallen off or been thrown out of the plane. Days without an archaeology.

Maddy touches each one of the objects in her museum case. After she touches the last one, the bone, she brings her fingers back to her lips and kisses them. Then she flops backwards onto her narrow bed, pushes her face up against the cinematic Grace O'Gorman on the wall beside her pillow. She shivers as the cool, shiny paper of the photograph presses delicious against her warm skin.

"Why aren't *you* my mother?" she asks.

WILLA LOOKS DOWN over the side of the plane to where waves scribble a loose calligraphy on the island beaches. The flat of sand is punctuated with driftwood and moving dots that are most likely people. The small world, thinks Willa. That's how it seems to her now, what's down there. Far away and filled with miniature activity that is becoming less and less comprehensible. What do they do on earth she wonders as the Moth draws an invisible curve over the eastern gap. What could possibly keep people interested enough to want to stay down there?

Do you remember your life? she writes on the warm back of Grace O'Gorman, the sun showing up the dirty white cotton of Grace's shirt as Willa carefully prints the letters.

Grace motions for Willa to take the stick, turns round and signs a response. The words flicker in the twilight like the wings of a slow bird.

This is my life.

She turns back to flying the plane and Willa leans back in her cockpit, head against the padded leather collar of the fuselage. If it weren't for gravity, she thinks, no one would stay on earth. Up here earth is in its proper perspective, small and distant. Beautiful, yes, but so much detail that people's focus must get scattered. They can't see their own lives. They can't see the shape of what they live — that rib-curve of sandbar, that stutter of islands.

Willa has to pee. The awkwardness of pulling her pants down to her knees, of sliding the enamel pot under her, has become easy and familiar now. The worst part is still the dump over the side of the plane, when sometimes the wind will carry a splatter of urine back against her face. It's all right today though. She sloshes the chamber pot with disinfectant and stows it down beside her seat. Sometimes when Grace pees she passes the pot back to Willa so that Willa can empty it. Where Grace sits in the front cockpit there's the wings and wires beneath her; it's harder to get a clear shot at the ground.

All the airborne survival acts have achieved a routine daili-ness that has replaced their counterparts on earth. Willa finds it hard to remember ever wanting to do something such as cooking. What could she possibly want to make? Here she just eats what gets lowered in the canvas supply bag. Some days she's hungrier than others and the event of eating is often more exciting than the food itself, but there's no real effort or thought involved and it doesn't seem to require more. The meal is low-ered and unwrapped and portioned out and eaten. Simple.

So much of what people do on earth seems a complete waste of time. Filling their days until they die, thinks Willa grimly, with meaningless ritual and a false sense of their own importance. The world does not care, she thinks suddenly. The world that we live in and give our lives to does not care for us at all.

They are flying at twenty-five hundred feet. Willa finds that she no longer has to look at the altimeter or the airspeed indicator. She knows within a hundred feet how high they are and she can tell, almost to the number, how fast they are travelling. She feels the Moth now as if it's her own skin — every graze of wind, every beat of the engine is acknowledged, felt, measured, every change in rhythm is noted and judged. The Moth wings fibrillate in a gust and Willa feels her own heart quiver in her chest.

Living completely outdoors all these days has taught Willa a lot about the way the world plays itself out on the human body. She knows the parched lethargy of too much sun, the way the rain's insistence sometimes makes her feel like crying. She knows that between three and five in the morning the body crawls into a cave and, if forced to be awake, operates in a numbed stupor. By 5:00 A.M., when the sun is up into the sky, the body feels awake and alert again. She knows that partial exhaustion is almost painful, but that total exhaustion feels quite calming and peaceful. She has watched the measured pace of the sun's arc and the more dramatic, less predictable rising of the bloated or famished moon. She has felt the stars on her upturned face and the clumsy fumbling of the wind. She has tasted bad weather on the roof of her mouth. She has worn a mantle of heat and suffered the lashing of storms. Punishment. Reward. This comes and that goes. Fickle, fickle sky.

It's around seven o'clock in the evening. Willa can tell by the way the sun is curling its tendrils in, pulling back into the horizon. In less than an hour it will drop its bulk down behind the water.

No wonder people used to believe in the edge of the world.
Flat earth.

She never gets sick of the landscape of Grace O'Gorman
— the smooth hill of her head, the ridge of shoulders. She
never gets tired of the way she skates over muscle and bone as
she writes on Grace's back. The feeling of skin, the way it cau-
terizes the words that drip from her hands.

But don't tell her, she thinks. Don't mention love. Be
careful. Willa has no way of knowing how much Grace
already senses about what Willa feels. Just as Willa feels the
plane as part of her body, she feels Grace that way, can sometimes swear she feels the casting and reeling in of her
breathing. Grace is in the plane with Willa, therefore Grace
must be feeling some of the same things. This is the base of
all Willa's theories, this secure, indisputable fact of shared
experience, gives her faith. If she is going mad, then Grace is
going mad too, but Grace doesn't seem crazy, so perhaps
Willa isn't either.

There are things Willa can ask her partner. The easier questions.

Are you cold?

Doesn't it look far away?

And there are things she just can't bring herself to say.

Could you love me?

But maybe Grace is experiencing the flight differently. A
lot differently? A little? How to grade the increments of indi-
viduality. Does Grace experience things in another order?
Surely the colours and shapes of what can be seen below will
be the same for both of them. But maybe they do see different

things altogether. Maybe everyone invents the world in order to describe it to someone else.

Do you see the coal hills?

Yes.

Do you see the dark slick channel tongue?

Yes.

Can you feel me?

Yes.

IT'S EVENING. Del and Fram sit at the kitchen table in their house, untouched bowls of soup in front of them. Del is dressed in regular clothes, out of her sickbed nightshirt, and has both feet propped up on an empty chair. The kitchen window is open and the lake can be heard quieting itself against the shore of the bar. Simon leans up against the counter and tells his story.

"Yesterday night it was. Started as a simple ball game. Thought I'd wander over to the Pits to see the boys play. Jewish men's team against a Gentile team, usual thing. It was a fairly hot day, remember, but evening was just starting to rub a bit of coolness in and Christie Pits is one giant bowl of a park. Always a little cooler down in there.

"Mixed crowd. Young guys I see around the neighbourhood — Jews and Italians, the Gentiles all sitting together in a clump as if they're scared to sit beside a Jew in case they become one. Disease, isn't that what they say about us overseas? Anyway, nothing too bad is happening. Some comments, three people chanting that song. The Jew song. To the tune of 'Home on the Range.' I don't sing so good, but it's like this:

Oh give me a home where the Gentiles may roam,
Where the Jews are not rampant all day;
Where seldom is heard a loud Yiddish word
And the Gentiles are free all the day.

"I know, I know, disgusting shit. And not even a good rewrite — 'day' rhyming with itself. Don't they have the imagination to think up another word that could go with it?

"So, anyway, I'm sitting there, ignoring the Gentile supporters, talking to some of my friends. And that's all fine. Nice night for a ball game. And it is a good ball game. But we lose, the Jewish team loses. And that's what I don't understand. We lost the game, why did they get all hot about that? It was when everyone was leaving the park, walking up the steep grassy sides of the pit to get back to the streets. A group of Gentile boys started yelling insults, then climbed up onto the roof of the clubhouse and opened this big banner with a swastika painted on it. The police found it later in a neighbourhood garage. It was a blanket. A blanket with a swastika symbol. That was all it took. The Jews leaving the park swarmed the clubhouse to get the Nazi boys. The baseball teams got involved because they hadn't left the field yet. Everyone was beating everyone else up. A riot. What the papers say is true, it was a riot. A lot of yelling and confusion. People running after other people. At one point I was more afraid of getting trampled than getting jumped or hit.

"It went on for a couple of hours, I think. Scattered out into smaller street fights. Cops arrived. No one I know got hurt badly, some bruises and cut lips. Loose teeth. Maybe it was more serious for some others but the boys I know are mostly all fighters anyway, or belong to street gangs. They know what to do to protect themselves.

"Me? I knocked a couple of boys down who came after me, but mostly I was trying to get out of there. I wasn't mad, I guess that's what it was. I saw that Nazi sign unroll against the sky and it didn't grate on me like it did on some of the others. I don't know why but I just thought it was stupid more than anything else. I wasn't prepared to be angry. I didn't want to fight. Too much like work, that's what fighting is. I'd just come to watch the ball game and enjoy the evening. I'd just come to sit in the stands with my friends."

MADDY PREPARES Miro's bath. She heats water on the stove in four separate pots, carries each pot with a towel wrapped around the handle to the large porcelain tub and dumps it in. She pours cold water in from a bucket at her feet, refills the bucket from the kitchen sink, pumping water in with the hand pump on the counter. She lugs the pail back to the bathroom, sloshing water on the floor as the heaviness knocks against her legs. She stirs the water with her finger, trying to decide how hot to make it.

Miro is at work, on display in his living room. The bay window serves as his showcase. There's a blanket hung behind the alcove so that the public can't see right into his living quarters. When on display he rolls around on several large pillows, shakes his rattle and sucks on a giant bottle that is sometimes filled with whisky and milk, sometimes just plain milk. If it's hot, he'll just wear a diaper. In the cooler weather he has various outfits that he dresses in — a sailor's suit, a one-piece bathing costume, a white christening gown. The gown confuses some people, makes them think that he's a girl wearing a dress. Today, Miro is just in a diaper, lying back on his pillows, pushing half-heartedly at a coloured beachball with his toes.

When Maddy calls him for his bath he waits until there are no people pressing their ugly faces against the window, rolls off the pillows and props a Back Soon sign up against the glass.

"God damn zoo," he mumbles as he waddles into the bathroom. "Tapping on the glass like this is a monkey house." He stands still as Maddy unpins his diaper — which is really a tablecloth — and folds it over the back of a wooden chair by the toilet.

"And they're cheap little buggers," he says, lifting one slow leg up and over the bathtub rim, leaning back on Maddy for balance. "No metal rain in the box today."

"Maybe they're tired of you because you're always the same," says Maddy, pushing him over the side of the tub and into the water. "You're always a baby. You never grow up."

"As if I could," says Miro. "They'd be expecting the King of All Fat Babies to grow into a towering giant. That's logical. Not some stunted dwarf who's the same size as the fat baby. Impossible." He leans back and the water laps up against the island of his belly. "Maddy," he says. "The trick is to not start off in the wrong place. Will you wash my head? I like it when you rub hard."

"All right."

Maddy sits on the edge of the tub and bends over to reach Miro's bald head. She can feel the little prickles as she soaps it from where his hair is growing back. To keep himself in a baby-like condition Miro has to shave his head almost every day.

"That's nice," he says, his eyes closed as Maddy vigorously rubs a white film over his head. She makes a cream, draws two lines in it, rubs them out and traces a capital *A* onto Miro's skull.

"Feel that?" she says.

"Yes."

"What is it?"

"The letter *A*."

Maddy smooths the soap back into an unbroken surface and writes a word carefully on Miro's scalp. "Feel that?"

"Grace," he says, eyes still closed. "Ah, your dream girl. Grace O'Gorman, Queen of the Skies. Still up there?"

Maddy retraces the soapy name with her finger, etching it deeper into the layer of foam. "I think she might be my mother," she says.

"Your mother?" Miro opens his eyes. "You already have a mother. Who would want two?"

"Well," says Maddy, not sure that she should tell him, but there's no one else she can tell and all day the knowledge has been exploding out of her. "I found something."

She steadies herself by pushing on Miro's head with one hand while the other digs a piece of paper from her pocket.

"A while ago I wrote to Grace O'Gorman and now she's written back. I found it on the road on the bar. Almost right outside my house." She unfolds the paper by shaking it out and holds it up to Miro's face.

"It's a newspaper," he says.

"No, look." Maddy shakes it in front of his nose. "There are words in pencil. A note." She reads it out. "'I love you,' and it's signed 'Grace.' Why would she tell me that if it wasn't true?"

"It is a bit strange," admits Miro. "But it doesn't make her your mother."

Maddy flutters the newspaper again. She feels her heart stuttering in her chest. "Don't you see," she says. "She couldn't say 'Mother' on the note or else I wouldn't know who it was from. She had to sign her real name."

Miro is quiet for a moment.

"Maddy," he says, "what about your other mother? Del. The one who lives with you."

Maddy refolds the note against her chest, using one hand. "She is just keeping me," she says, stuffing the piece of paper back into her trouser pocket. "Until Grace is ready to come and get me and take me to my real life."

Miro lifts a hand out of the water and reaches up to Maddy's face. He gently traces a line around the perimeter of her face — forehead, cheek, chin, cheek, forehead. He lays a wet finger against her lips and she lets him.

"Oh, Maddy," he says softly.

She sucks at his finger.

The water tastes soapy.

The flesh tastes sweet.

GRACE FALLS ASLEEP at the controls on the morning of the next day. She slumps forward, her body half over the stick, half against the side of the cockpit. Willa has to use all her strength to pull the plane out of a suicide dive. It's just like one of Jack's stories, she thinks, one hand on Grace's collar, one hand on the stick. What was that line she liked? "A strength wrested from fear."

They don't have a sign for *sorry*, so the best Grace can do is shrug her shoulders and smile tiredly. She looks exhausted. Willa leans over and writes on her cheek.

Are you all right?

Grace shrugs her shoulders again, nods yes.

To prevent another disaster they alter the flying rotations from three-hour shifts to one-hour shifts. Now there can be no real sleeping, just dozing, but flying for one hour will not be as taxing as flying for three. It seems to work, though Willa is convinced that sometimes she is flying the plane while she is asleep. The one-hour-shift changes also lessen the distinction between the conscious and the unconscious world. It all becomes a hazy place of partial wakefulness, a state that approaches sleep from two directions — veering down towards it and floating up out of it.

When she's flying the plane Willa tries to find something to concentrate on in order to stay awake. During one rotation she focuses on the activity on the water below the plane. Two sculls spidering along the regatta course, a barricade of canoes either side of them. Practising for the big three-mile race on September 1, she thinks. Everyone in the city has money on this one. Willa plans to mob the bleachers on the lakeshore along with everyone else to watch the boats slide over the slick surface of the lake. She will put some coin down on Bob Pearce to win.

On another circle over the harbour she watches the tall spikes of the *Lyman M. Davis*'s masts. It would be nice to see them threaded with sail, to see the huge wooden schooner moving from its anchorage. Does it notice? she wonders. Does it feel the difference between staying in one spot and plunging through the fitful seas?

The Moth gives a little cough and Willa jerks out of her contemplation. Another kick in the engine and then it becomes a regular miss in the beat. The cylinder's not firing properly again and this time it hasn't corrected itself. The cylinder's on the way out. It could go fairly quickly — within the day, or it could last until the end of their flight. As long as it's just misfiring and doesn't go completely dead.

Grace turns in her seat and makes the sign for *plane* and then the sign for *down*.

Willa nods, *I know*. She pulls the throttle back, slowing the plane's speed. Still the ticking from the front of the Moth. She pushes the throttle forward, increasing the speed. Still there. It's obviously not going away. Another thing to add to the list of "wait and see." Wait and see if Jack sabotages them in the final stages of their flight. Wait and see if they go mad from lack of sleep. Wait and see if their bodies cease to function, or cease remembering how to function. Wait and see if the cylinder goes dead and they have to land. Every halo they make around the harbour seems to add another complication to their lives.

Willa has lost track of the days they've spent in the air. She's too busy worrying about potential danger to remember if it's Thursday or Friday. She tries to keep a record of the number of days they've been flying but she thinks she might have missed one somewhere along the way and she's not sure now if they've been up for eighteen days or seventeen days or nineteen days.

How many days? she writes on Grace's back after her one-hour shift is over.

Grace holds up her hand four times — three times with all the fingers spread, once with only three fingers up. *Eighteen*. Willa is not convinced that Grace's sense of time is any more reliable than her own. She used to look at the dates on the newspapers that Jack sent down, but he hasn't done that for a few days now and she's lost count of when the last delivery was.

What if they don't know when to come down?

This day, whatever it is, is warm and cloudy. A little wind from the north, nothing to cause any trouble or discomfort or affect their fuel consumption. The refuellings go well. They eat cheese sandwiches for lunch and an apple afterward, tossing their cores over the side of the plane in unison.

In the afternoon Willa has stomach pains. Her first thought is that Jack has poisoned the food and she will now die from that cheese sandwich she enjoyed so much. When she doesn't die she is willing to consider other possibilities and decides that perhaps what is happening is that she's getting her period. She thinks that her last period was just before they took off, but she can't be sure. She can't be certain of anything that happened before the flight, that happened on earth. Her memory for that life is unreliable. Just when she's convinced herself that she is about to have her period, the pains subside and she realizes that it might just as well be indigestion, not cramps. Why can't she tell what's happening to her body? Is it like the schooner, if it's not moving then it doesn't exist in the same way anymore, it's not itself?

Do you feel sick? she asks Grace, and Grace shakes her head, *no.*

Do I look all right to you?

Grace twists in her seat, one hand still on the stick.

Yes.

Grace reaches out and pats Willa on the cheek to reassure her, then turns back to flying the plane.

When it's her turn at the controls again Willa resumes her new method of concentration, focusing on something she's flying over. She looks at the roofs of the buildings in the C.N.E. She looks at the ship traffic in the port, tries to see the cargo that's being unloaded from each vessel. She watches the people on the beach at Sunnyside, little dots on the sand and in the shallows. She watches the shiny black tops of the cars on the road. She tries not to fall asleep. She tries not to fall asleep. She tries not to fall asleep. She . . . tries . . . not . . . to . . .

"I THINK I WANT a door this time," says Del, walking around the stacked platforms of wood on the ground. "A real one that opens and closes. And locks."

Fram rests back on his heels, a hammer in his hand. "We can be doing that," he says. "Save you locking that junk away at night in that metal trunk you were having in the hut."

"Junk." Del walks around behind him and cuffs him on the head lightly. "You watch yourself, Fram Stewart, or I'll be telling your future."

Fram grins. "This is my future," he says, raising the hammer and knocking another nail into the boards.

Maddy watches her parents from inside the carousel, astride her favourite horse, Amelia. The carousel is silent, too early in the day for anyone to want a ride.

Fram and Del are building a new fortune-telling booth so that Del can go back to work for the weekend trade. Tomorrow is Saturday and the biggest crowds are usually at Hanlan's on a Saturday. To be ready for the weekend Del has had to buy new cards and candles. The crystal ball was salvaged from the fire, a little smoky but the cloudy glass should add to its mystery, should be an asset.

Maddy has been asked to help with the construction. She has been offered the job of nailing on the tin stars and moon that Fram has hammered out of a bit of stovepipe, but she has refused to have anything to do with a new fortune-telling booth. She sits on the wooden horse and remembers the fire, the way the tin stars flashed through the darkness like a code, the still figure of Del on the ground. She doesn't understand why they would want it to happen again. The men in the circle. The flames. The smell of burning wood. Maddy is sure that the new hut will meet the same fate as the old one. And what if worse things happen to Del this time? The men who'd beaten her had never been caught. They might come back. Maddy doesn't believe her parents and Simon who tell her that it's over, that it was a once-only thing because of Simon's fight. She doesn't believe them when they assure her that there's no reason for it to happen again. Maddy knows better. They're not facing the truth. To her it's simple. Del was beaten because she's Jewish. *She's still Jewish.* The men weren't caught. They could come back. She spends some of her time now looking for them. Riding round on her bike at dusk, checking who's coming off the ferry at Hanlan's. Somebody has to be aware of what's happening, and if her parents are being so stupid, then it has to be up to her to stop the next attack.

"Hey, Maddy," calls Del from outside the carousel. "Come and help us with the walls."

Maddy squeezes her legs around Amelia's girth. "No," she yells back.

"Come down here," orders Fram.

Del touches his arm. "Leave her be," she says.

They don't ask her again.

She watches as they nail two walls together on the ground and then push them upright to attach the third wall. The wood is clean and new. Fram knows someone at a lumberyard and traded the wood for his labour, fixing one of the sawmills. "Only the best," he'd said to Del as he and Simon lugged it off the ferry. "We'll be doing it right this time."

Maddy looks at her parents and thinks that she can't possibly belong to them, either of them. They don't look like people who have a twelve-year-old girl. She's never thought of them as young, but today in the soft afternoon light they seem that way. There's a quickness to their movements and they're playful with each other. It makes her feel lonely.

Perhaps even her father isn't her father.

Ever since the fire there's been this new thing between them. A lightness. Maddy remembers Fram's reaction the night of the fire. How he ran from the carousel, and all the way home his face was a stiff mask to keep from crying. How he looked after Del when she was resting upstairs — bringing her food and things to read, talking soft to her all the time. Maddy has even seen them kissing, not once but twice; and they lean into each other all the time as though they can't keep their balance. The more she stares at them, the more unfamiliar they become.

Stupid, thinks Maddy from the safe height of Amelia's back. They've become stupid.

She had expected that after what had happened to Del, Fram would refuse to let her continue as a fortune-teller. But this was just another place where they reunited. Instead of dissuading her from starting over, he encouraged it. There wasn't even much discussion, just an agreement to rebuild the hut. And they didn't even tell Maddy until after Fram had brought back the wood, as though they assumed she'd feel the same way they did.

Maddy lies forward on Amelia and wraps her arms around the cold, hard neck of the horse. I'm not yours, she thinks and just then hears the plane that carries her real mother pass overhead. It sounds different, something in the engine has changed. She listens carefully as the Moth flies south above the islands.

Fram and Del have fastened the third wall onto their structure. At this point it looks like a packing crate, not a small building. Shipping me off, thinks Maddy. That's what they'd like to do. Send me away so they could be happy like this all the time.

THERE'S A STORM in the night. Rain shovelled hard back in their faces by a strong wind, skeletons of light dancing over the dark water. They keep the plane low to avoid the sting of rain against their skin.

Rain at night is Willa's least favourite thing. There's the reduced vision and the discomfort, the chill and the gloominess of being soaking wet in the clinging dark.

Grace and Willa are still keeping to their one-hour rotations, but when the storm starts at 2:00 A.M., neither of them rests for the remainder of the night. Willa slouches into her jacket, performs the convulsions necessary to get into her oilskins and hunches back down in her cockpit to wait the rain out. She doesn't wear goggles or a helmet. Even though goggles are protection against the rain, they make it hard to see anything, and she doesn't wear her helmet because when it's wet it sticks to her head like a plaster cast.

This storm, though there doesn't seem to be as much rain as a few days ago, seems worse. It's the angle of the rain, Willa decides. How it comes straight back from the engine, a sharp, searing blade. The propeller helps to slow the onslaught, but not enough to really help.

All right? Willa writes on Grace's back. It must be twice as bad for her, sitting up in the front of the plane.

Grace nods, *Yes.*

Just before dawn, as the rain filters out into a fine misted spray, the engine goes dead. Willa is flying the plane over the lake from Sunnyside towards the islands. It all happens so quickly, so slowly. There's the sudden change in noise, the air pouring past the fuselage and the moment it takes her to realize what's missing from the landscape of sound. She feels it physically, a hard blow to her stomach, her breath knocked out of her. She throttles down and up again. Nothing. The blades of the propeller swing lazily around, limp and dangling in the air. The Moth, only at twelve hundred feet to begin with, is losing altitude. It seems to take forever for Willa to tell herself that the plane has to be landed. There's no time to glide it around and over to the Air Harbour. Already she can see the veins on the surface of the lake. The trees on the island seem level with the plane. She has to keep the Moth flying straight, not have it go into a spin, spiralling down to crash. Willa feels a disbelief, a slow, opening panic at what is happening. Suddenly there's resistance on the stick.

Grace has taken control.

The ailerons are down, the flaps jackknifing the air to slow the speed of the plane. Grace is heading for the sand beach on the western bar. It looks clear except for some knots of driftwood up by the tree line. Willa's body has stiffened, rigid hands grasping the edges of her cockpit. Magneto, she thinks. Probably got wet from the rain and shorted out and all the time we've been worried about the cylinder. She hears the whistle of the wind in the rigging wires. She sees the back of Grace's head, the rising water, the slow tick of the propeller turning nothing over.

Grace slides low over the lake. They skim the rind of blue and Willa realizes that they're too low. Without thinking she grabs the stick, pulls back to lift the nose of the plane and try to lengthen the glide so they make the sand. The sun is just beginning to stain the beach with light. Willa feels the fuselage scrape along the top of the water. She still has her hand clamped around the stick when they crash into the lake.

———————

Her first thought is that they're floating. The plane sits on top of the water, she can feel the nudge of the waves against the hull. She shakes her head.

The Moth is parallel with the beach. It must have twisted when it hit the water and spun to face south. The nose is up, almost above the water and it's the tail that must have hit first. Willa looks behind her and sees a tangle of wire and a fin showing beneath the surface. The fuselage just behind her cockpit is partially submerged. The wings seem bent but still intact. The rigging wires have snapped and dangle from the upper wings like stray threads from a coat.

There's an unbelievable silence everywhere.

Nothing hurts.

Grace.

She's lying forward, over the stick. She doesn't move when Willa grabs her shoulder.

Grace.

Willa opens her mouth to speak her name but nothing comes out. She tries again. Her mouth opens and closes on air.

From somewhere on shore there's the trill of a bird.

It's dawn.

Willa tries to unlatch her port door but the latch is jammed. She pulls herself up and, holding onto the upper set of wings, climbs shakily out of the cockpit and stands on the lower wings. She reaches into Grace's cockpit and hauls her backwards off the stick. Grace flops sideways and Willa sees the blood on her face, the gash above her left eye. She scoops some of the lake into her hands and tosses it into her face. Grace opens her eyes, looks right at Willa and opens her mouth. No sound. Willa lifts an arm and wipes some of the blood from Grace's forehead with her sleeve. Grace looks dazed, opens her mouth again, closes it.

No words.

Willa slowly lowers herself off the wing and into the water. They have to get away from the plane before it sinks. She puts her leg down. Down and hits the bottom.

The plane isn't floating, it's stuck in sand. The beach must taper out slowly. They're in shallow water, the water is just past Willa's knees. She sloshes around a little just to make sure that it's not a sandbar, that it's really this deep all the way in to the beach. Her legs feel disconnected from the rest of her body, almost absent. She has to keep looking down to make sure that she's still walking and hasn't wobbled over and collapsed.

She wades back to the Moth and tugs on Grace's arm. Grace is half under the front section of the plane, yanking at something in her storage compartment. She pulls out a black box.

The barograph.

Willa hadn't even thought of rescuing the barograph. Without it there's no official recording of the flight. Without it they won't know how long they were in the air and whether they did break the record or not. Grace puts the barograph carefully into her canvas rucksack and passes it out to Willa.

Grace has trouble standing as well, falls back twice and has to be half dragged out of her cockpit. Her legs don't work either and the fliers stumble slowly through the water towards the beach, Grace's arm around Willa's shoulders. She leans on the younger woman, is pulled along. The rucksack with the barograph is strapped to Willa's back.

There's a rush of wings, a cloud of birds lifting from the trees. Willa looks up and sees a young girl standing at the water's edge. She has her hands stretched out towards them as though their stumble through the water is some kind of baptism, as though her hands are raised in blessing.

"I've been waiting for you," she says.

FRAM AND DEL are sitting at the kitchen table when the door opens and Maddy, who they thought was still in bed, enters with two women right behind her.

"These are the pilots," she says as they collapse through the doorway. "They don't talk."

The pilots are slippery yellow. Rain, thinks Del slowly. There was rain. She and Fram rise in unison from the table and give the women their seats. Del notices the smell of unwashed flesh as the one nearest her crumples onto her chair. One of them is cut across the head. They have the hollow eyes of soldiers.

Maddy stands by the counter. "Wash her," she says, and Del thinks, rain. Blood. She wrings a towel with water at the sink and stands over the one with the wounded head.

"It's all right," she says as the woman flinches from her touch. "I'll just clean it up. See how bad it is. It's just water I'm using." She gently towels the woman's forehead and the woman closes her eyes.

"Where did you come from?" asks Fram, addressing the one who isn't hurt. "Should we be getting things from your plane? Should I be doing something?" he asks doubtfully.

"They don't talk," says Maddy. Her eyes are fierce and Fram feels completely at a loss with these two crashed women in his kitchen and a daughter who seems to know what they want when no one else does.

"Where did you find them?" he says to her.

Maddy has her eyes on Del and the wounded pilot. "They crashed," she says. "I woke up not hearing their plane and I went looking for them. They crashed just off the bar."

Fram looks out the small kitchen window as though he'll be able to see the plane from the house. He sees the sun rub the tarnished grass across the road.

"We'll have to get them to the mainland," he says. "Their people will be anxious for them."

Maddy rocks back and forth on her heels. "No," she says. "They're mine. They came for me."

The woman whom Del is tending opens her eyes and looks at Maddy. She seems about to say something, but stops before any words leak from her lips. She snakes her hand through the air and the other pilot tries to stand up.

"Why don't they talk?" says Fram. These women unnerve him. Their faces are dirty and red from the sun. Their hair is filthy and there's a wildness to them that makes them seem unnatural, not human.

Maddy doesn't answer him.

"You need someone to look at your head," says Del to the woman she's bent over. "I can't get it to stop bleeding. Maddy." She looks up and over to her daughter by the sink. "Go upstairs and fetch me another towel."

Maddy hesitates and then reaches down and grabs the

hand of the unhurt pilot. "You come with me," she says. "There's things I need to show you."

The woman struggles to her feet and follows the girl slowly up the stairs.

Maddy's bedroom is dark as usual. The pilot stumbles over something on the floor and almost falls. Maddy rips the curtain away from her window and light spews into the room. She pulls the pilot over to her bed, to the small table beside her bed.

"Here," she says. "Look. These are yours."

Willa looks down and sees a wooden tray filled with what looks like garbage — an apple core, a piece of metal, an old newspaper. The light polishes a shape on the wall and she sees that it's a picture. Grace. She has to get back to Grace. She has to get Grace back to the city.

"No, wait," says the girl as Willa lurches for the door and staggers down the stairs.

Maddy stands in her room, almost listening for the plane and hearing instead her father's voice from below.

"We'll take you to the ferry."

"No," she wails and plummets down the stairs, banging into the wall at the bottom.

Everyone looks up.

"Where's the towel, Maddy?" says Del, and then there's silence and they all look away.

MADDY WALKS between Grace and Willa, through the amusement park to the Hanlan's Point ferry docks. Del and Fram follow, under Maddy's pleas, about thirty feet back. Grace holds a towel to her head with one hand and Maddy holds onto her other hand, guiding her to the docks. Willa wears the canvas rucksack. They move slowly through the empty park, passing the bulk of the refreshment pavilion, Miro's small bungalow. They walk by Del's new booth and the tin stars glitter like shiny coins in the morning sun. They walk by the carousel with its wooden horses frozen in full gallop, flick of foam in their teeth.

"You did come for me, didn't you?" says Maddy to Grace, but the aviatrix doesn't answer or look down.

The ferry waits beside the dock. Maddy walks with them right onto the boat.

Grace O'Gorman drops her hand and turns away, her eyes as blank as the eyes of the carousel horses.

"Didn't you come for me?" says Maddy, feeling more and more uncertain about Grace's intentions.

The famous aviatrix, Grace O'Gorman, looks annoyed, waves her hand to Maddy to shoo her off the boat.

"You broke the record," says Maddy desperately and Grace swivels back towards her and smiles weakly. "Nineteen days," says Maddy.

She stands there for a moment, waiting for Grace to grab her, to say something, to smile again. Willa Briggs seems to have fallen asleep, head leaning back on the wooden deck railing, rucksack cradled under her right arm.

Grace O'Gorman adjusts the bloody towel on her head, waves Maddy away again and then seems to forget her completely, looks out over the water towards the buildings of the city.

The ferry horn blows.

"Maddy," calls Del from the end of the dock.

Maddy doesn't move. She looks at Grace O'Gorman. This Grace has never cared for her, didn't come here to rescue her. The Grace Maddy was waiting for doesn't exist, or she's still out there, somewhere up above, circling.

Here Maddy is, this August day, standing on the solid steel deck of the ferry. Behind her are the islands. The early-morning sun, whispery trees, these are real. Her parents waiting at the end of the dock. This is where she comes from, who she is.

"Maddy," calls Del again.

And Maddy turns away from Grace and moves home towards her mother's voice.

FRAM AND DEL stand at the end of the dock, watching Maddy on the ferry with the pilots.

"Fram," says Del quietly. "When I was washing her head, Grace, the famous one, I felt something from her." Del watches the wind blow a piece of paper along the ground. "She was supposed to have died in that crash."

"What?" Fram turns to her, the question tearing slowly out of him.

"Grace O'Gorman was supposed to have died in that crash," repeats Del firmly. "It was her time to go. I felt it."

"But she didn't," says Fram.

"No."

Del can see the two pilots slumped against the side of the ferry, two yellow spots against the thick lines of the rails.

"She didn't die because two people needed her to be alive. Two people kept her alive by needing her."

"Maddy," says Fram softly and turns to his daughter's stiff figure on the horizon.

"But you can't cheat your fate," says Del. "This time there was Maddy and the other pilot. Next time they won't be there."

"Next time?"

Del watches the yellow oilskins until they blur into the sun. "What was supposed to happen today will happen anyway. The next time Grace O'Gorman flies will be the last."

They are silent. The crew on the ferry are getting ready to haul in the heavy mooring lines.

"Maddy," calls Del.

GRACE LOOKS at the towel. Not so much blood. It seems to be stopping. She presses it back against her forehead. Up in the wheelhouse she can see one of the ferrymen talking to another excitedly. They look down at her and Willa. One of them points.

This is it, thinks Grace. This is the moment before we are noticed, the moment before we are really back on earth. She feels in her shirt pocket for her lipstick. Soon there will be crowds and photographers, reporters asking mindless questions. "Do you feel disappointed that you crashed?"

No.

If that strange little girl was right, the one who found them, then they *have* broken the record. They have flown a perfect line across the sky. "That's what matters," Grace will say to the flashbulbs and idiot grins. We did it. And there it will be, all over again. The adulation. The letters from children who want to grow up to fly and the letters from adults who wanted to but didn't. Grace O'Gorman lives everyone's dreams for them so they don't need to have any.

And there will be the next flight to prepare for. The next record. Maybe solo distance. Fay Weston is challenging

Grace's existing record next month. If Grace times it right, she could take the record back the day after Weston breaks it. She has to keep her name in the news so she can keep flying.

And then Jack will have to be forgiven, both publicly and privately — though perhaps not right away. But she can't keep blaming him for disappointing her. He can't help it. It's not egoism, it's the truth — no one can keep up to Grace O'Gorman. The only way she can be assured of people trying to keep up is to have them fall in love with her. Then they will make the effort and be able to maintain her high standards temporarily. And what do they fall in love with, anyway? Air Ace Grace, Queen of the Skies, the image they've created and bought into.

And you too, thinks Grace, looking over at Willa sleeping. You fell for me too. For it. I made you.

The wind channels along the deck and the weight of it against her face makes Grace feel comforted. It feels like being in the plane. Her poor old Moth, stuck in the drink. They'll have to haul it out. No small job, salvage. Dry out the engine. There'll be the newspaper and magazine pictures in the plane, beside the plane, in the water replaying the moment after the accident. *Adventure Girl.* Now at least she'll be able to take that stupid logo off the fuselage.

"Do you remember the crash?" they'll ask.

No.

But suddenly Grace does remember. The surprise of feeling Willa override her judgement and wrench back on the stick. *No one does that to me.* She remembers the loud sound of nothing and Willa's face in the wrong place.

"Did she save you?"

No.

Grace raises a hand to shift the towel on her forehead and her fingers catch the wind, twist a shape in the air, a word.

Fire.

Well, yes. Maybe she did.

And not because I made her love me. Made her fly like that. We talked. There was more to say up there because we couldn't say it. There were days when I just wanted to give her a new word. Only that. Just one. And she understood what I meant. I didn't make that happen.

Sky.

Earth.

Remember me.

I'll remember you.

Grace peels the words from the air, both hands working, the towel on her lap. There was a reach to this that felt exactly like flying.

"Can you talk about what this was for you?"

Yes. I can.

Remember me.

But I won't. Not to the flashbulbs. That's something not for the public.

Grace stretches across and shakes Willa gently by the shoulders.

"Wake up, Willa Briggs," she says. "I've got something to tell you."

AUTHOR'S NOTE

In the early 1930s, individual exploit was encouraged in North America as a form of escapism from the economic depression. Aviation was championed as a new phenomenon and pilots who completed noteworthy flights were often met on the ground by thousands of supporters. The popularity of flying extended to, and was embraced by, women as well as men. In spite of the novelty, record-setting pilots such as Louise Thaden, Ruth Nichols, Bobbi Trout (not to mention Amelia Earhart) were also considered genuine heroines of their time.

Leaving Earth is a work of fiction but the historic details of the era, flight, mechanics and particulars of 1930s aviation are factually based. Most of the events and incidents that occur in the story are documented historical happenings within Toronto in August 1933. The places mentioned did exist — the Air Harbour, C.N.E., Hanlan's Point Amusement Park. The sign language used in this book borrows conceptually from the gesture language of Native North Americans and from monastic sign language.

The flight in *Leaving Earth* is modelled on one made by American pilots Frances Harrell Marsalis and Helen Richey, who flew a Curtiss Thrush over Miami, Florida, from December 20 to 30, 1933, setting a national endurance record.

A year after the Miami flight, Frances Marsalis, a renowned aerobatic pilot, was killed during a solo air race in Dayton, Ohio, a race that Helen Richey then went on to win. In 1935, Helen Richey became the first female commercial airline pilot but was forced out within the year by objections from the less-experienced male pilots on staff. She later obtained her instructor's licence and was the first woman to train military pilots. After the war, with the return of the male pilots from overseas, she was unable to find work in aviation, and in 1947 Helen Richey took her own life. She was thirty-eight years old.

Women such as Marsalis and Richey are largely forgotten now, their achievements distilled, simply, into the legendary figure of Amelia Earhart.

I have used some technical detail from the Marsalis–Richey flight but I have not attempted to replicate the women themselves. I only hope that in *Leaving Earth* I am able to capture the very real sense of flight as passion and vocation that these and other early women pilots lived.

ACKNOWLEDGEMENTS

I am indebted to the following institutions and individuals for assistance during the research of this book: the Ninety-Nines, International Organization of Women Pilots; Michael Moir at the Toronto Harbour Commission Archives; City of Toronto Archives; Linda Cobon at the C.N.E. Records and Archives; Canadian Warplanes Heritage Museum; International Women's Air & Space Museum; Environment Canada.

For their generosity and support I would especially like to thank the Toronto Island Airport Flight Centre, de Havilland Inc., and the National Aviation Museum in Ottawa.

I am grateful for financial support from the Ontario Arts Council and the Toronto Arts Council received during the writing of this book.

For support, technical advice, editorial suggestions, and for listening to me talk incessantly about 1930s aviation, I would like to thank Mary Louise Adams, Elise Levine, Su Rynard, John Kalbhenn, John Barton, Carol Malyon, Catherine Vernon, Matthew Fairbrass, and Amy Willard Cross. Special thanks to Frances Hanna.

Thanks to Phyllis Bruce for her editorial care and acumen.

Leaving Earth owes a particular debt of gratitude to the American aviatrix Bobbi Trout, who, among her many accomplishments, has the enviable distinction of being the first woman pilot to fly all night. I am grateful for her support and advice during the writing of this book, but most of all I am grateful for her continued friendship.